he **Preacher and The Prostitute**
maica Treasures Book/February 2012
Published by Jamaica Treasures
Kingston, Jamaica

ork of fiction. Names, characters, places, and
either the product of the author's imagination
titiously. Any resemblance to an actual person
iving or dead, events, or locales is entirely
coincidental.

ISBN - 978-976-95287-6-5
Jamaica Treasures Ltd.
P.O. Box 482
Kingston 19
Jamaica W.I.
www.fiwibooks.com

Maribel sighed, "I   g,
Pastor Edwards."

Brian laughed, "Don't Pastor Edwards me, Sister Contrell."
He glanced at her. "Call me Brian."

"Well Brian, people are not always all they seem to be."

"That is a loaded statement that I want to pursue with you
later." Brian nodded. "So where in Jamaica were you living
before Kingston?"

Maribel glanced at him. He was driving along asking
questions which on the surface were so simple, but to her
were such a big part of the barriers that she had placed
around herself to protect her new identity and to forget about
the past. Here he was tearing through her barriers and doing
so quite cheerfully.

"Maribel?" He glanced over at her tense expression. "Is it
top secret?"

"Oh … no … I was born in Westmoreland. Grew up in
Negril."

"Negril?" Brian glanced at her. "You didn't say a word
when I was telling you about my grandmamma. Do you
know I still have family there? Maybe one day you and I can
take a drive down there."

"No!" Maribel shouted. She could feel herself getting very
agitated at the mention of such an idea. She would not be
going back to Negril even if her life depended on it.

THE PR

THE PR

BREND

A J

ALSO BY BRENDA BARRETT

Di Taxi Ride and Other Stories
The Pull of Freedom
The Empty Hammock
New Beginnings
Full Circle
The Preacher And The Prostitute
Private Sins (Three Rivers)
Loving Mr. Wright (Three Rivers)
Unholy Matrimony (Three Rivers)
If It Ain't Broke (Three Rivers)
Homely Girl (The Bancrofts)
Saving Face (The Bancrofts)
Tattered Tiara (The Bancrofts)
Private Dancer (The Bancrofts)
Goodbye Lonely (The Bancrofts)
Practice Run (The Bancrofts)
Sense Of Rumor (The Bancrofts)
A Younger Man (The Bancrofts)
Just To See Her (The Bancrofts)
Going Solo (New Song)
Duet On Fire (New Song)
Tangled Chords (New Song)
Broken Harmony (New Song)
A Past Refrain (New Song)
Perfect Melody (New Song)
Love Triangle: Three Sides To The Story
Love Triangle: After The End
Love Triangle: On The Rebound

ABOUT THE AUTHOR

Books have always been a big part of life for Jamaican born Brenda Barrett, she reports that she gets withdrawal symptoms if she does not consume at least two books per week. That is all she can manage these days, as her days are filled with writing, a natural progression from her love of reading. Currently, Brenda has several novels on the market, she writes predominantly in the historical fiction, Christian fiction, comedy and romance genres.

Apart from writing fictional books, Brenda writes for her blogs blackhair101.com; where she gives hair care tips and fiwibooks.com, where she shares about her writing life.

You can connect with Brenda online at:
Brenda-Barrett.com
Twitter.com/AuthorWriterBB
Facebook.com/AuthorBrendaBarrett

Prologue

"**F**lash up yuh lighter!" the selector yelled over the microphone.

It was early Sunday morning and the dance, which had begun at eleven the night before, was just heating up.

Several persons, mostly male, milled about the street; most of them were clutching drinks in their hands and smoking. The air was redolent with the scent of tobacco and marijuana mixed with the aroma of spicy jerk chicken.

The pulsating beats of heavy dancehall music rocked the early morning air as paid dancers and other partygoers writhed to the heavy beat. Some dancers were spurred on by the obscene commands of the selector and they attempted gravity-defying dance moves, to the pleasure of their street-side audience.

Maribel loved the freedom of it all. There was no time to self examine and to feel pain at a party like this; she flung a hunk of her blonde wig over her shoulders and licked her lips suggestively at the selector.

He grinned at her; she was a regular dancer, one of the local girls from Negril that they hired to dance at local street dance sessions that they held in small communities across Jamaica.

Her eyes were slightly glazed and she swished her hips seductively in his direction. He felt in his pockets to see if he had any loose change and then shrugged his shoulders at Maribel, pulling out his empty pockets for her to see.

She smirked at him and then turned away disinterestedly, looking in another direction—she never spoke to guys who had no money, and he knew this well.

He laughed and shouted into the mike, "Big up to Peaches, the hottest gal in the dance tonight."

Maribel turned around and smiled at him, holding up her empty plastic cup. He winked and indicated to the bartender at the makeshift bar to fill up her cup.

Maribel headed toward the bartender, feeling slightly tipsy. She had to fight off several groping hands as she made her way to the bar. Her sheer top and boy shorts, both in hot pink, proved to be too much of a temptation for the drunken party goers scattered throughout the street; they groped her exposed body every chance they got and whistled and hollered at her to give them some attention.

It gave her a rush to know that whenever she came to street dances she was generally the focus of the male attention. Her honey-gold skin, paired with her usually outlandish wigs, was a real eye-catcher, and if her current patron was to be believed, her eyes were brown orbs of seductive mischief.

She laughed out loud, lost in her inner musings, and danced up to the bar, happy that her work for the night was finished and that she could just enjoy herself at the party.

"Peaches, you is a real sexy woman, y'know," said the

bartender admiringly. His black eyes gleamed with rampant lust.

Maribel hissed her teeth and held up her cup. "You can't afford me."

She watched him as he poured the liquor in the cup and then a soft drink, just the way she liked it.

"I used to know you from before … " the bartender grinned, "back when you used to sell your body for $500, on the side street at West End in front of Pete's shop. I could afford you then."

Maribel inhaled sharply, her hands trembling; she hated being reminded about the last two years. She thought of it as ancient history, when she bothered to think of it at all. The things she used to do didn't make good memories.

The music sounded like it was coming from afar and she shook her head as she stumbled away from the bar.

"Peaches, you all right?" asked the bartender as she retreated. The drink sloshed over the rim of the cup as she used one hand to steady the other.

She staggered to an empty spot near a couple that were grinding and gyrating against a wall. The female, who was in a short tight green dress, was trying to emulate a new sexual position that was gleefully suggested by the sound selector.

She closed her eyes and tried to block out the couple beside her and the memories from her past. Every time she thought that the past was truly behind her it seemed to rear its ugly head again. She rested her drink on top of a concrete block and sat beside it gingerly.

She had to remind herself that she was better off now than back in the days when she was forced to leave home by her abusive father, whose disciplinary measures involved beating her until she could not walk. Her sister had been unable to take the abuse and had run away from home, leaving everything behind, and at sixteen, after becoming the sole recipient of her father's brand of abuse, she had followed.

She hadn't dared to go back because she knew that her father would have killed her for sure. He had gotten more violent in the last days leading to her escape. At one time a neighbor had to hide her under a bed until he had calmed down sufficiently to listen to reason—her infraction that day was that she had reached home from school five minutes late.

Her father's main mission in life, after her mother and sister had run away, was to turn her into a true lady of upstanding character. He often said he wanted to eradicate any lingering character traits of her sister and mother that could be found in her, and his favorite weapon of eradication was his half-pound belt. The ugly thing had blunt studs fashioned in the center of the worn black leather and would leave bruises and scars on her body for months.

After leaving home she had survived for a while by living with a man, but his wife soon found out and she was kicked out on the streets once more. For a time she was lost and lonely in Negril, with no one to turn to, but then she met Felicia, whose street savvy had rescued them both from one scrape after another.

When Felicia had suggested that she take up a street name for her seventeenth birthday, she had agreed and from then on she was called Peaches. It was also Felicia who had determined that they were both too pretty to be street-side whores.

"We should be earning much more from better-looking men," Felicia had announced seriously. The next day she signed up Maribel to star alongside her in a porn video. One video became two and before she knew it she had starred in a grand total of fifteen videos.

Maribel jerked out of her reverie as she heard the selector screech, "All the women, who know that them have them own man, put up your han' in the air."

Women were waving their hands all over the place and shouting. Maribel got up shakily and accidentally upended her drink. She looked at it dazedly, wondering how on earth she was so happy just fifteen minutes ago and was now so unnerved by the blasted bartender's comments.

Felicia had always insisted that she should grow a backbone. Well, Felicia wasn't here right now, was she?

Tears were welling up in Maribel's eyes as she took off her shoes and walked past the selector and the sound boxes onto the warm asphalted road. The music was loud and she could feel the pulsating beat of it in her own heart rate. The sound boxes were stacked so high, they looked like hulking black specters in the night.

She winced as she passed the little groups of men standing at the side of the road leering at her suggestively; she ignored the catcalls and whistles and went toward the taxi that she had earmarked to take her home.

It was a fifteen-minute drive to Negril's West End, where she lived with an American national called Jim. She only saw him for four months of the year when he visited Jamaica and fondly referred to him as her sugar daddy, a role he was quite happy to fill. He didn't ask her many questions and she did not ask him any. She lived in his cottage and was ostensibly his house sitter; he trusted her enough with the responsibility to pay the housekeeper and gardener, and basically keep his house in one piece. In return, he had a bed partner when he was in Jamaica.

She tiredly grabbed the handle of one of the car's doors and the taxi man, who had been snoring lightly around the wheel, jumped up confusedly. He saw her shrugging on the sweater that she had left on the back seat and sat up, coughing.

"You ready?"

"Mmmm," she muttered noncommittally. She wanted to leave, but at home there were only memories and emptiness.

"Why are you crying?" the taxi man asked, looking at her glassy eyes through the rear-view mirror.

She sniffed, "Today is my twentieth birthday and the anniversary of my best friend's death."

The taxi man, looking slightly taken aback, pulled out of the cul-de-sac where he had parked and slowly pulled out onto the main road.

"Well, erm…happy birthday, I guess."

"Thanks," she said impatiently. She didn't want anybody to feel sorry for her.

"How come your friend died on your birthday?"

"Got shot at a party."

"Oh." The taxi man looked thoughtfully back at her. "I would feel afraid of parties after that."

Maribel hissed her teeth. "Without parties, what do I have? I am a dancer. I have to dance; partying is my job."

"Well … there must be something else you can do," the taxi man snorted. "Most people have more than one skill. I can cook, so I used to own a cook shop."

"I have other skills," Maribel snapped. "I was good with mathematics and accounts, but that was before I left school."

After Felicia died, Maribel had to take responsibility for tidying up her accounts and paying her bills, a chore which had revealed that Felicia was not the poor street urchin she had pretended to be. Instead, she was a wealthy young woman in her own right, and she had left all her money to Maribel—money that Maribel still had difficulty using. Maybe, someday, when she was not as raw with emotions from Felicia's sudden death, she would consider it, but for now she drifted from party to party, feeling empty and alone.

"You shouldn't have left school," the taxi man mumbled. "Men like good-looking women for a while, but they prefer the intelligent ones who can challenge them for long term."

He guffawed when Maribel shot him a dirty look.

"Men are not interested in me for anything else but my looks and how I can please them in bed."

"Sometimes you have to do something other than pleasing men," the taxi man said philosophically. "You should probably make an effort to do something to enhance those brain cells that God gave you, and go back to school! Perhaps you should go get some peace at church ... now that would be something."

He grinned as Maribel screwed up her face and cringed. "I am not into no God business," she rebutted quickly, pleased to see her house in the car's headlamps. "God has never done anything for me yet."

The taxi man took the money she shoved at him and watched as she scrambled out of the car.

She hobbled in her pink high-heeled shoes toward her gate; her short clothes and daring hairstyle made her look so vulnerable to him—like a lost little girl just turned twenty and probably lived a lifetime already. He shook his grey head.

The morning was clearing up as he glanced at the dashboard clock; it was five-thirty and a cool breeze was blowing from the sea in the distance.

"Listen Miss," he shouted from the taxi as she turned around to close the gate, her mascara running as tears fell freely down her face.

"You might not think you need God now, but my granny used to say that it's the people who think that they don't need him that really do."

She gave him the finger and strolled up her walkway, slamming the front door behind her.

Chapter One

Five Years Later

Maribel sat at the front of the church, bobbing her head to the music as the choir sang. It was Wednesday evening and it felt strange to be sitting in a church with empty pews, but she had vowed this year, after being in the church for three years, that she would be participating in church activities, and after sitting beside the choir mistress one Sabbath, she was ordered to join the choir.

"Meeting begins at five sharp," Sister Claudia had said to her sternly. "I detest it when people who should know better waste their God-given talent. You are wasting your lovely singing voice."

Maribel had nodded bemusedly. The well-spoken Sister Claudia had always reminded her of a stern principal and so she had always felt a little nervous around her. She spoke with a crisp British accent and carried herself upright and had a firm, no-nonsense voice. She wore a tight bun and had well-plucked, finely arched eyebrows. Many of the church folk were unsure of her age; she just seemed timeless.

Maribel focused on her as she agilely played the piano.

"That's enough." She turned to the choir, thirty individuals who were attired in their work clothes and looking pretty tired.

Maribel's friend Cathy, whom she had met at University and who was instrumental in bringing her into the church, winked at her.

Sister Claudia, whose face was set in stern lines, glared at the group. "Ladies and gents, our choir is an award-winning choir. Unfortunately, this evening you are sounding like you have never gotten an award."

Everyone murmured their assent, looking sheepishly at each other.

She picked up her director's stick and walked slowly across the platform in front of the choir loft. "The garbage that passes for music today, even if it is religious, has spoiled your musical ear. We need to go back to the times when real music stirred the senses and brought glory to the Savior. We can well do without the hauly-drauly drivel that I hear passing for gospel music, accompanied by screeches and screaming that must, I am sure, make our dear Savior wince."

The choir chuckled.

She cleared her throat. "I want us to sing *Worthy is the Lamb* with all the parts: soprano, alto, tenor and bass. Sister Maribel sings the most heavenly soprano I have ever heard and I am grateful that she has graced my ancient ears with her wonderful voice."

Some members of the choir giggled.

"Silence." Sister Claudia looked at her brood reproachfully. "I am in the mood to extend practice tonight."

You could hear a pin drop as the threat sank in. No one wanted to stay longer than usual for practice, and they did not take Sister Claudia's threats lightly. The Saints of Christ choir was an award-winning outfit and highly respected both locally and internationally. Choir membership was considered a privilege, so no one dared to jeopardize his or her position.

Maribel edged closer to the end of the seat as Sister Claudia turned to her. "Well Sis Maribel, let us hear how well you can do."

"Deep breaths," Maribel whispered to herself. She glanced at Cathy, who gave her a thumbs up.

Okay, here goes. She stood up and thought to herself, *Okay Lord, you want me to glorify you with my singing talent, so sing with me.*

She closed her eyes and sang. *"Worthy, worthy is the lamb ... worthy, worthy is the lamb ... that was slain."*

After she finished the last high note, which was no real effort for her, the choir clapped.

"Well, well," Sister Claudia said happily, "Sister Bertram, make space for Sister Maribel beside you, in the first soprano section."

Maribel heaved a sigh of relief; she felt such a sense of accomplishment that she had made it that she had to laugh inwardly. There was a time when she had been bold to show off her body, or her seductive dance moves, but while she was auditioning for a church choir she had been as nervous as a cat on hot bricks. She moved toward the sitting choir members and sat down beside stout Sister Bertram.

Who knew that the girl from Negril, who had told the taxi man that God had nothing to do with her that long-ago day, would be first soprano on an award-winning choir? She smiled and thanked the Lord for his mercies.

When they had a break from the surprisingly tiring practice, which was partly due to Sister Claudia's perfectionism, Sis Bertram walked up to Maribel, smiling.

"Sister Maribel, I am so happy that you are actively participating in the church services."

Maribel nodded; she was finally feeling as if she belonged after sitting in church for over two years doing nothing. At first she had been afraid to interact with anyone. She feared that they would sense that she was a fraud and did not belong with righteous people. Her only friend in church for several years was Cathy, and this was so because she knew her from her university days.

Cathy had taken her to a church crusade, which was held near the school. Maribel had only gone because it was her birthday and that year she was feeling lonelier than ever.

She had gotten several party invitations to various clubs from her regular party crowd, but then her roommate, Cathy, had announced that she was going to the biggest and best party around. Maribel had gone more out of curiosity than anything else because she hadn't known Cathy to be a party girl.

It turned out that she went to the crusade in a mini skirt and a skimpy top and came back with a Bible and an invitation to go back.

She tuned in to Sister Bertram and saw that the lady was looking at her with a faintly impatient air. "As you know, I am the head of the Women's Ministries Department at our church."

"I didn't know," Maribel replied.

"Didn't know that I was the head?" Sister Bertram looked hurt.

"No, didn't know that the church had a department called the Women's Ministries."

Sister Bertram looked a bit mollified by that admission. "Well, the previous leader only allowed her friends to join," she looked peeved at this declaration, "and she kept the department like a friendship club, so I am not surprised that you don't know about it. Let me tell you, it's a department that caters to the special needs of women in our church. We pray for each other and share our advice as women and friends. We are like a women's support group."

Maribel nodded, fascinated.

"We meet every Sunday morning at seven. You can bring a friend—female, of course. We have breakfast afterward and share our hopes, dreams and aspirations. All secrets are safe with us."

Maribel smiled and thought silently, *Not my secrets.*

"I will come this week," Maribel said, smiling as Sister Bertram clapped her hands and grinned.

It would be good to know the women in church and to make more friends. There was nothing better than a female support group, or so she had heard. Some of the men had already tried to chat her up and she had not been exactly blown away by their approach.

Besides, whenever she thought of relationships her past reared its ugly head. Would she have to confess her past to a future husband? Perish the thought; no docile church brother would be comfortable to know that she used to be a prostitute.

Sister Bertram turned to somebody else who demanded her attention, patted Maribel's hand and walked away.

"What was that about?" Cathy sidled up to her and asked.

Maribel glanced at Cathy and laughed, "Sister B wants me to join the Women's Ministries."

"Didn't I tell you that when it rains it pours?" Cathy hugged her. "I am so glad you are participating in church.

Church participation strengthens your faith and gives you that extra impetus to come to church and share with the brethren, even if you don't want to."

Maribel rolled her eyes, "I hope she doesn't expect me to share my deep, dark secrets and cry into my tea at these meetings."

Cathy smiled, her big brown eyes lit up in glee. "Don't even think about telling them that when we met I had to bribe you to come to church."

Maribel smiled. "And that I was in a skimpy skirt and sheer top, thinking that I was going to go to a huge party, or that my sugar daddy had rented a hotel for us to spend the weekend and I had just come back from said weekend slightly drunk."

Cathy laughed, "You were indeed the worldly roommate from hell."

Maribel sighed. "But God can change a worldly roommate into an exemplary church sister, can't He?"

Cathy nodded. "Exactly. A word of warning, though: some people only go to the meetings to hear the business of others, so keep the confessions to a minimum. Even though most church people mean well, there are some who will hold your past against you and make attending church that much harder."

Maribel nodded vigorously. There was no way on earth anyone—not even Cathy—would know about her real past. As far as she was concerned, Peaches and her colorful history were dead and buried, and from that Maribel had arisen.

Chapter Two

The Women's Ministries meeting was in the dining hall on the second floor of the church building. Some women still had on their tie-heads and what looked like their nightgowns. Cathy waved to her and patted the empty chair beside her when Maribel peeked through the door.

"I didn't know dressing was so casual," Maribel whispered to Cathy when she sat down. She felt overdressed in her pink skirt suit and heels.

Cathy slapped her hand on her forehead. "I forgot to tell you to dress as if there are no men around."

Maribel eyed Cathy's jeans and oversized t-shirt. "Right."

They sat in a semi-circle as Sister Bertram cleared her throat to begin.

"Ladies, we have a special guest this morning." The ladies smiled at each other. "As you well know, this church is a big church with over six hundred members, 60% of whom are ladies. We ladies need to stick together like the women who used to follow Jesus. Their names are not as widely known as the men's, but they were there and their work was relevant."

There were nods all around.

"Sister Maribel," she paused, "please introduce yourself to your sisters in Christ, so that we may no longer be strangers to each other."

Maribel got up smiling. "My name is Maribel Contrell."

The sister to the other side of her started laughing. "I am sorry." She held up her hands when everyone, including a frowning Maribel, looked at her.

"Sister Thelma, please," Sister Bertram said, pained, as Sister Thelma tried to bring her mirth under control.

"I am only laughing because of the rhyme. Maribel Contrell! The next word should be hell. Maribel Contrell, who came from hell, is looking well." She hooted some more and then wiped her eyes. "Just a little Christian humor."

Maribel looked at the malice in her eyes and had to stop herself from shuddering. She had never met this woman; why did she dislike her so much?

"Well ... erm ... my name is Maribel and I am an accountant."

"Where are you originally from, Maribel?" a kindly middle-aged lady asked. "You look very much like the wife of a nephew I have in St. Elizabeth. With your golden-toned skin and big brown eyes, you two could pass for at least cousins."

Maribel smiled, "I am from Westmoreland." She didn't want to give them her exact address; that would be delving a little too close to her past for comfort.

The sister nodded and smiled.

Maribel sat down and glanced at Cathy. She badly wanted to ask her about the laughing Sister Thelma with the malicious eyes.

"She may be nice looking but she doesn't hold a candle to my Rose," Thelma hissed so that only Maribel could hear.

Maribel swung around and looked at her, but she had pasted on a phony smile.

Amidst the welcomes and the handshakes from the women in the circle and the warmth with which each woman introduced herself, Maribel could feel Sister Thelma's poisonous regard. She was filled with an unshaken certainty that this woman was a loose cannon and would prove dangerous to her peace of mind.

"Well, we have several new items to discuss this week," Sister Bertram said brusquely. "The new pastor was introduced last week. As we all know, he is coming from a Canadian church; he is bright, well-spoken …"

"Handsome," one sister piped up quickly as she twirled her hair dreamily.

"Hot," her neighbor said quickly.

"Single," one old lady pointed out gleefully.

The other sisters started whispering to each other and Sister Bertram tried to talk over the din. She held up her hands. "Okay, all right. He is handsome, hot and single, but he is the Lord's man."

"And will soon be mine," Sister Carlene's voice bellowed over the drone of voices, as she got up and flicked imaginary lint off her long-sleeved floral dress. "Let it be known, youngsters and grannies, that man was sent by God for me specially. God has heard my thirty-five years of prayers. I have kept my body pure as the driven snow, kept lustful thoughts to a bare minimum and you could insert my name in Proverbs, where Solomon talks about a virtuous woman. I have been doing my best for the Lord's cause and he has sent me a juicy reward: the perfect man in the form of Pastor

Brian as an answer to my prayers."

"He is thirty," Sister Thelma said snidely. "He wouldn't want you; you are too old. On the other hand," she held up her hand as Sister Carlene was about to protest, "my Rose is perfect for him. She just completed her MBA, magna cum laude; she is merely twenty-five, has the looks, and will match him perfectly. And she will be coming to the next Women's Ministries meeting," she finished smugly.

Carlene sat down, defeated. The specter of Rose was obviously a huge one and Maribel longed to see who this paragon of virtue was.

"Well, if you are going to volunteer Rose as future wife," Sister Greenland said, her quivery voice piping up through the many whisperings, "I am going to throw into the ring all my twenty granddaughters who are coming to this church. Men are at a scarcity in this place, so if Rose wants him she has to fight for him, and can I say that all of my grandchildren are educated and attractive."

Sister Bertram placed her head in her hands and shook it. "Ladies," she looked at them, pained, "I wanted us to make plans for the pastor's welcome dinner on Thursday night, not fight over who the Lord sent him for or who is perfect for him." She glared at them. "Anyone hearing you bicker would think you are man-hungry beasts on the rampage."

"A dinner is a great idea," Sister Greenland said, sounding pleased.

"I will bake my famous corn pone," one church sister said happily.

"I am going to do my special jerk chicken," Sister Carlene said, pleased that she was once more in the running for the pastor's affection.

"He doesn't eat meat," Sister Bertram said, placing a damper on that suggestion. "I asked him, and he said no meat and no sweets."

No meat? No sweets? What is this? How does he keep so buffed looking? The whispers grew to a crescendo.

Sister Bertram held up her hands once more. "I have the menu planned; I just need volunteers for the following dishes …"

As she announced each dish she was bombarded by volunteers.

Cathy whispered to Maribel, "I forgot how entertaining Women's Ministries meetings could be."

"They all seem so human," Maribel said in awe. "Behind the church dresses and polite smiles, this is what happens?"

"Not all the time." Cathy shifted in her seat and glanced around, checking to see where Sister Thelma was. "The pastor being young, single and hot has resulted in all the gloves being ripped off."

"I wish I had been here last Sabbath," Maribel said morosely, "then I could see what all the hullabaloo is about. Is he that good looking?"

"Succulent," Cathy said, licking her lips.

Maribel gasped, "So how come you didn't tell me?"

"Each sistah is on her own," Cathy said, laughing and looking at Maribel's expression. "I didn't tell you 'cause I forgot. But obviously now, I must. He is a tall chocolate bar of pastorly goodness."

Maribel snorted. "Seriously."

"Well seriously," Cathy said, jumping when Sister Thelma pushed her head between the two of them.

"I am disappointed in you, Sister Cathy. I thought you were going to marital counseling with that nice Brother Norwood."

"That doesn't mean I cannot look," Cathy said defiantly. "Where in the Bible does it say, 'Thou shalt not look at another attractive man ever again once you are engaged to another'?"

Sister Thelma ignored Cathy and looked at Maribel and asked, "How old are you, dear?"

Maribel looked at her distrustfully; her voice was dripping with honey, a sickeningly sweet tone that sounded so insincere that Maribel found herself involuntarily wincing. "Twenty-five in another three months."

"Ah," Sister Thelma said thoughtfully, "and yet I can see that unlike my Rose, you have probably lived a very colorful life."

"Why would you say that?" Maribel demanded, her heart picking up speed. Did this lady know her from somewhere?

"It's just that you haven't been in the church long," Sis Thelma snorted. "You are fairly attractive; who knows what you were up to?"

"What's her problem?" Maribel asked Cathy, feeling really mad as the church sister looked at her smugly.

"Jealousy," Cathy whispered. "She had the pastor earmarked for her precious Rose and then here you are—a threat."

"But why me?" Maribel squeaked, partially relieved that Sister Thelma didn't seem to know a thing about her, and mad that she couldn't confront her in the way that she wanted to.

"Look in the mirror," Cathy giggled. "If you weren't a sanctified church sister I would hazard a guess and think you would be in modeling, or something along those sultry lines."

Maribel subsided in her chair. She couldn't argue with that. At one time she had been into nude modeling, and much worse.

The meeting concluded with a prayer session. The women gathered in a circle but Maribel was quite reluctant to hold

Sister Thelma's hand, whose face had now morphed into sanctimonious lines. She held Maribel's hand in trembling fervor and Maribel watched as she closed her eyes and silently whispered in fervent prayer.

They were asked to share their prayer requests with each other and share in what aspect of their lives they most needed God's intervention. Sister Bertram had stressed in a little pre-prayer speech that there was power in numbers, and that the effectual fervent prayer of a righteous woman availeth much.

The prayer request started with Sister Bertram, who was doing her CPA exams. "Please pray for me as I take my exams tomorrow."

Everyone nodded in commiseration.

"Please pray for me that I find myself a husband," Sister Carlene said coyly.

Everyone snickered at this. Maribel especially found it impossible to hold back her mirth and she was shuddering with silent laughter when it was Cathy's turn.

"Please pray for me; I get married in five months," Cathy said and squeezed Maribel's hand.

"Please pray for me. I have a very demanding boss who is testing my faith," Maribel recovered enough to say.

"Please pray for my son Gunther," Sister Thelma said as she gripped Maribel's fingers tightly. "He is playing in the devil's den with pornographic videos, his filthy dancehall music, and his refusal to come to church and read the Bible."

Maribel felt a twinge of sympathy for Sister Thelma, as there seemed to be tears in her eyes, and then she continued, "And pray for my Rose, who has done well with her degree and is about to start her job as Managing Director in a very large company. And pray for my husband; he has to choose between a white SUV and a one-year-old black BMW. The choice is important to us, as we are changing the paint in our garage. Amen."

Cathy's shoulders were shaking beside her and Maribel could see that others were not wearing a serious expression as they listened to Sister Thelma's prayer request.

She was too astounded by the blatant bragging to even react. What was even more baffling was that Thelma still had her eyes closed and the pious expression that she had earlier adopted firmly fixed to her face.

Sister Bertram paused a long moment after that request and as they bowed their heads and hummed a prayer chorus, she finally opened her prayer by saying, "Lord, remind us now of the true meaning of Christianity and help us to leave self behind as we approach your throne of grace …"

Chapter Three

Maribel whimpered when the clock alarm pealed. She was not looking forward to going to work today. She dragged herself out of bed and looked in the mirror, but the pink suit from her Women's Ministry meeting was draped across the glass, obscuring her view.

It was a little quirk of hers to look in the mirror first thing in the morning. Felicia used to joke that she was making sure that she was still in one piece.

Even to herself she looked apprehensive this morning. She moved closer and looked in her brown eyes. Was that fear?

Was she fearful of going to work this morning because of Mark Ellington? Last week he was promoted to being her boss, and that promotion would come into effect today. To say that they had a very tough working relationship would be an understatement.

Mark had mastered the art of subtle sexual harassment to perfection. He never broke any rule but there was a very definite something in the air when she came near him and now that he was no longer an ordinary colleague, but her supervisor, she could just feel her sweat glands getting ready to work overtime.

She actually felt a cramping of fear in her stomach. She stumbled and sat back down on her bed. It was only six o'clock; she had two hours to get ready.

"Okay Maribel," she whispered, "when you gave your life to Christ you believed that He would be true to his word. He said in Matthew 6, 'be anxious over nothing.' Let's make this day a practicing Christian day. Today you are going to practice what you read in the Bible. Fair enough?" She glanced at herself in the mirror again. Her reflection still looked worried.

Only prayer will do this one for you, my girl—on your knees. She fell on her knees and started praying. When she got up she felt so much lighter and more positive, to the extent that she hummed through her breakfast of yogurt and fruit.

She hummed when she took out her red power suit. She hummed when the neighbor in the apartment above hers blocked her in and she had to knock him out of bed to move his car. She hummed though she was stuck in traffic and reached work one minute after eight.

"Maribel, you have started the week in a very bad way." Mark was standing in the lobby when she entered the building. A cup of coffee was in his hand and he had a grin on his face. "I would report you to your boss if he wasn't already here to witness it."

The receptionist, who had just come in behind Maribel, rolled her eyes and walked past Mark quickly. Maribel felt the feeling of euphoria she had after the prayer die a sudden death.

"Morning Mark." She forced out a strangled greeting.

"Morning," Mark said, clipped. "I asked Vivian to work with you on the Fowler account. I promised Graham Fowler the finished product in three days."

"But you can't do that, Mark," Maribel sputtered. "I work directly with that account, I know exactly what is involved, the case load is a very complex one, plus I have other cases. Three days is too short for me to finish that account, even with help."

"You'll manage," Mark said sardonically. "I have every confidence that Fisher and Smith hired you to this accounting firm because of your competency and not just because of your good looks." He said it with a question as his eyes crawled over her suggestively.

Maribel cringed at the blatant look of lust in his eyes. The look reminded her so much of the past and how she used to revel in that sort of attention; now it left her feeling nervous and dirty.

She knew she was a good accountant; she had a very good head for figures and had passed her ACCAs and accounting degree with flying colors. She comforted herself with the fact that the company's head, Mr. Fisher, would not have hired her if she weren't very competent. The firm was too big, and their reputation too important, to ruin with the hire of an airhead beauty.

Mark knew that and was only being rude and degrading to let her know who was in charge. His weak and mean attempts reminded her of a schoolyard bully who only wanted to show that he was bigger and meaner than everyone else.

The implications of what he had done finally hit her as she contemplated it. She brushed by him as he stood in the passageway leading to the offices.

She had to work flat out on these accounts. She could

forget sleeping and eating for the next three days. *He did it deliberately, the worm.* She was not one of the women in the office who was bowled over by his handsome looks and phony charm when he had just arrived at the branch, and he had never forgiven her for that.

She couldn't quit the job now, she thought feverishly as she entered her office. The world of accounts was a fickle one; she had just been working at Fisher & Smith for seven months. Any employer after this one would wonder why she would leave such an impressive world class firm without a solid reason.

She couldn't tell them that her supervisor looked at her like a sex-starved maniac and dropped innuendos to her when he was sure that nobody else would hear. It would be her word against his and the evil sicko would probably tell people that she came on to him.

She sighed and ran a hand through her hair and then realized that she had caught it up in a bun this morning, in an attempt to look stern, bookish and ultra professional. She was trying to go with the Sister Claudia look but she had still gotten the slimy once-over from the rotten critter.

I hate him.

Then she turned on her computer monitor and saw the thought for the day on the screen: 'Beloved, let us love one another, for love is of God and everyone who loveth is born of God and knoweth God.'

"Lord, I am sorry, I don't hate Mark. I detest his personality pretty strongly."

"Talking to yourself?" Vivian stuck her head through the door.

"Yes," Maribel said, disgruntled. "Have a seat. I was just told by our very august boss that you and I are to work on the Fowler account for the next three days. It looks like we'll have to live here for the next couple of days, in order to meet the deadline."

"You lie," Vivian gasped. "Why would he do that? Fisher and Smith are all about quality, not haste."

"Well, my thinking is that he wants me to fail," Maribel sighed. "For some unexplained reason Mark Ellington has a fascination with me. I have been here for seven months and was quite happy until they transferred him from the downtown office. Since then, he is always giving me suggestive looks and his conversations are always steeped in sexual innuendos."

Vivian gasped, "He is so handsome. I think he is a bit taken aback by your aloofness."

"Taken aback is a mild phrase compared to the passive aggressive, tacky sexual undressing looks I get from him." Maribel shuddered as she opened the file drawer and searched for the Fowler folder.

"You should report him," Vivian said decisively.

"And say what, that Mark looks at me like a starving man about to devour a plate of food?"

"That might not work," Vivian said thoughtfully. "Abigail in Human Resources has this thing for him and might think you are exaggerating or worse, lying."

"Found it," Maribel said, pulling out the file and returning to the overflowing desk. "Okay, here is what I will do. I will try to clear up all of these by lunch time," she gestured to the desk. "I suggest that you do the same to your desk and then meet me in the conference room, and bring your laptop. We need to work for the rest of the day."

"What about the Mark issue?" Vivian said, standing up.

"I will pray about it, as I do about everything else, and the Lord will take care of it."

"Or you could get married," Vivian said jokingly, "and

put to rest the rumors going around the office that you are a lesbian."

Maribel smirked. "I will get married when the Lord sends Mr. Right. As for the rumors, I hope you put them to rest when you hear them."

"Of course." Vivian rolled her eyes. "I know that you are a Christian woman on the wait. Like so many …"

"Lunch time … Vivian," Maribel cut in impatiently.

Vivian laughed and walked through the door.

Pastor Brian Edwards. Brian glanced at his nameplate on the door and entered the spacious vestry that adjoined the secretary's office at the back of the church. He felt a tingle of anticipation, even though he had only accepted the job to pastor the church after long prayer sessions asking the Lord to show him the right decision to make. He had felt an almost compulsive need to come back to his parents' country—Jamaica—to do some sort of ministerial work with the people on the island.

The Lord had worked it out and he was offered the post as senior pastor for this church, while the previous pastor was heading for Canada to pastor the churches he had just left. It had seemed like an ideal swap at the moment, but he still had prayed about it just to be sure God was leading him to serve in Jamaica.

He had not gotten an earthshaking 'yes' thundered from heaven, but rather an urgent desire to work in this part of the world. He was enjoying the feeling.

He glanced around the office and left his briefcase on the desk. He would personalize it somewhat during the day. He knew that his vestry days would be pretty swamped with consultations from members who wanted private counseling sessions and others who wanted him to sign papers and do all manner of administrative duties. He already had five marriage counseling sessions scheduled from the previous pastor's diary, and he hadn't even properly met the members of the church yet. He knocked on his secretary's door and waited for her to answer.

"Come in."

She was talking on the phone when he entered, and he sat in front of her desk. She had several copies of church bulletins scattered across her desk.

"Coming, Pastor Edwards." She clamped her hand over the phone's mouthpiece. "I am on the line with Pastor Curry from Trinidad. He is scheduled to speak next month on family day; he is running his itinerary by me."

Brian nodded and whispered, "Take your time, and tell him I said hello."

She continued talking while he skipped through the church publication, quite awed by the number of activities that the church had going on. They had cooking classes on Thursdays; he made a mental note to attend. He was really helpless in the kitchen. He skipped through the publication and turned back to the congratulations section. A picture caught his attention.

"She's beautiful," he whispered to himself. She had fluffed-out shoulder length hair, which was thick and had hints of curls; her eyes were light brown and had an almost catlike curve. She had a button nose and soft lips, which looked as if they were painted the softest shade of pink. She had a vulnerable expression which hinted at an innocence he found touching. He stared at the picture so long that he had no idea that his secretary had come off the phone and was staring at him.

"That's the congratulations page," she said to him.

He cleared his throat and looked up. "So I see, Sister er …"

She laughed, "Sister Patsy Brown, sir."

"Yes, Sister Patsy." He had to remember that; where was his brain? He had seen beautiful women before; it was just that the picture had touched some unseen triggers in him. He suddenly felt his age and the fact that he was lonely and needed to find himself a helpmeet.

"Well Sister Patsy … I am sure we will work well together to further the Lord's work."

She looked at him hopefully. "Yes Pastor Edwards, I worked really well with Pastor Green. I only want to know if it's all right if my grandson Keron comes and waits in the office here for me on Tuesdays and Thursdays."

"Sure." Brian sat up. "I thought we had after-school care here."

"Yes, but Keron is a bit too hyperactive for the after-school-care helpers."

"Did you see your picture?" Patsy showed him the front of the publication with the headline, *New Pastor Comes to United Church.*

"Nice," he nodded, barely glancing at his picture. He turned back to the congratulations section and asked her, "Who is this?"

"Oh, that is Sister Thelma's daughter Rose."

Brian looked closely at the caption and frowned. "But this says 'congratulations to Sister Maribel for joining the award winning United Church choir. Keep on singing for Jesus.'"

"Oh, that picture," Patsy laughed. "I thought you were pointing to the larger picture."

Brian had barely seen the larger picture.

"Well, that is Sister Maribel Contrell; she recently joined the choir. According to Sister Claudia she has an angelic voice. I can't wait to hear her myself."

Brian got up, smiling. "I can't wait to hear either. Well Sister Patsy, I am off to sort out my office. I should be meeting one Sister Francine, who is supposed to drop off my house keys; she told me that she is the best housekeeper this side of Jamaica. Please send her through when she gets here."

Patsy nodded and he walked off, turning back for one of the copies of the publication. "Just to familiarize myself with the happenings," he said to her as she busied herself around the computer.

Chapter Four

"**I** can't believe we finished this monstrous pile of work."
Vivian looked at Maribel blearily. "What time is it?"

"Six o'clock," Maribel said tiredly. "It is days like these
that I miss coffee."

"Why don't you drink it?" Vivian asked, stretching.

"Has in caffeine," Maribel mumbled as she shut down her
computer. "Caffeine not good. Dehydrates your body." She
was talking in staccato notes and could hardly formulate a
thought. "I have to sing tonight at the new pastor's reception
my church is having."

"Okay," Viviene yawned, "I have been running on two
hour nights for the past three days. I don't even remember
what day it is."

"Thursday," Maribel yawned, and clapped her hand against
her mouth. "Did you hear my jaw bone crack?"

Vivian started gathering her things. "Yup, if it breaks you
can't sing tonight. I am so glad Peter dropped me off to work

this morning. I have to call him now to ask if he's ready. I couldn't imagine driving all the way to Portmore now." She fished out her cell phone from her handbag pocket and dialed the numbers quickly.

"Well," Maribel stood up and pushed her laptop into its case, "I told Monster Mark that I would be here at nine o'clock tomorrow, a full hour before the presentation to Mr. Fowler and his team, so I need to get some sleep after the reception tonight."

Vivian spoke in the phone quickly and turned to Maribel. "Paul is on his way. I can walk you to your car and wait for him in the parking lot."

"Okay." Maribel yawned again. "Can you imagine me singing amen ... yawn ... snore."

"Sing it for me," Vivian said as they headed through the door.

Maribel grimaced, "Let me just tell you that it was Sister Claudia's grand idea to have me singing lead with the choir doing backup."

Vivian laughed, "Your voice can't be bad if they are having you sing solo for the new pastor."

Maribel giggled as they entered the elevator. "I told Sister Claudia that I was going to be working late, so she said come at half past seven and then go back to work."

"Determined," Vivian said as the elevator doors closed, "now sing it."

"*Singing Amen ...*" Maribel crooned, "*Amen ... Amen ... Amen... now listen to a story ... is talking about my Jesus ... Amen ...Amen ...*"

Vivian was bobbing her head and humming. She followed Maribel to her car. "I absolutely wish I was going to be there," she said longingly as Maribel got behind the steering wheel. "You have a wonderful voice."

"Thanks," Maribel beamed at her. "After I leave here, I am just going to run to my apartment, have a quick shower, and jump into a simple red dress."

"Your favorite color," Vivian said smiling.

"And then I am going to grab a yogurt and some fruit."

"Don't forget to brush your teeth," Vivian said in a motherly voice and laughingly waved as Maribel backed out of the parking lot. "You will need your pearly whites to be gleaming when you sing *Amen*."

Maribel laughed and drove off. She played the CD with the song and wondered why Sister Claudia would have her singing a song with a choir that she had not even practiced with. What if she messed up and got tongue-tied or something? She pulled up in front of her apartment building fifteen minutes later, thanking God that she had not encountered much traffic; she barely had enough time to reach the church.

Brian knew the moment that she came into the church hall. The place was beautifully decorated with streamers and balloons. Tables were arranged around a head table where he sat with his church leaders and elders. The atmosphere was convivial, with some a cappella songs playing in the background. The church sisters were fussing about him, but there was nothing unusual about that; he was used to church sisters fussing.

And then she came in. Her face looked slightly flushed, as if she had been running. She was in a red dress, which fell demurely below her knee, and she was frantically looking around for somebody. He almost smiled when she placed her hand over her heart dramatically when she saw Sister Claudia.

He wondered if she was as beautiful on the inside as she appeared outwardly. If she was, surely she would have been married by now? No church brother would leave such a gem unspoken for. He sat, pondering her age, as the buzzing around him continued.

She looked to be in her early twenties, possibly twenty-three, he guessed as he stared at her fixedly. She was whispering something to Sister Claudia and licked her lips nervously.

He could tell that she was nervous because her eyes kept darting around the church hall, and then they rested on him. It was too sudden to glance elsewhere so he kept her gaze. Every sophisticated gesture that he knew and used to repel amorous overtures escaped his head. He wanted to act nonchalant and distant, not letting on that he liked her, but his gaze just helplessly clung to hers, the seconds ticking away slowly as his attention was caught in the brown orbs of Sister Maribel Contrell.

Maribel gazed at him; now she knew why there was almost a fight over him at Women's Ministries meeting. His face was beautiful, all the features of perfect symmetry, but it was his eyes … they were kind eyes; they drew her in, read her deepest thoughts, and then spoke acceptance.

She had to physically shake herself to turn away from the eye lock that they shared. She had never in all her years as a connoisseur of men felt such a connection with a particular man, and she hadn't even met him yet. She felt slightly exposed, nervous and vulnerable after that look.

She blindly staggered to a table and sat down. Her emotions were flayed with a look, her thoughts were in a jumble and a nervous pulse was fluttering in her hands.

"There you are," Cathy said, sitting across from her.

"Hey Maribel," Greg, Cathy's fiancé, said as he sat down beside her. "You didn't even give me a chance to act the chivalrous husband-to-be and pull out your chair," he said to Cathy.

Cathy snorted. "You successfully demonstrated your chivalry when you did not sit on the car horn when you came to pick me up."

Greg grinned and turned to a still dazed Maribel. "Why do you humans of the female persuasion take so much time to get ready?"

Maribel, struggling to get her fluttering pulse under control, tuned into her friend's conversation belatedly. "I don't take long to get ready."

She sneaked a peek at the pastor again to make sure that her initial reaction to him was not a fluke. She was sleep deprived and hungry; she could have imagined that intense eye lock.

She hadn't gotten to eat that yogurt after all, and the banana she had grabbed while she rushed to leave the house had not been very firm, so she had abandoned it in the car.

He was still there; his skin was deep chocolate, his head completely clean shaven and his beard and moustache neatly trimmed.

He was talking to one of the church elders and it was as if he sensed her regard; he looked up at the same time. This time he waved.

"Oh my," Maribel whispered, whipping her head around, and her eyes clashed with Cathy's. Greg was busy talking to a church brother beside him, but Cathy was looking at her knowingly.

"I knew it," she whispered, leaning toward Maribel. "I knew something was up when we came in; you didn't look like yourself. You like him."

"I don't …"

"Stop it, lying lips are an abomination unto the Lord and they that speak truly are his delight," Cathy said gleefully. "So go ahead, Sister Maribel, lie to me!"

"No, I … Well I … Cathy, this is ridiculous. I haven't even met him."

"Aha," Cathy said, glancing around and whispering fiercely, "but you don't have to. You are shaking. Praise the Lord, I am alive to see this; Maribel has finally rejoined the land of the living where men are concerned. Do you know that the last time I actually saw you in a relationship was that weekend when you left the school campus to stay with that guy—what was his name again? Oh right, Jim."

Maribel hissed, "Stop this Cathy, it was just eyes meeting across the room. Isn't the table set beautifully, and with fresh flowers, too?"

"I will allow the change of topic only because Sister Thelma and her daughter seem to be heading toward the two empty chairs around this table. I have got to find somebody … Sister Lily, you want to sit here with Carlisle?" Cathy yelled loud enough for Sister Lily and several other persons to hear.

"Oh yes," Sister Lily said ,waving and heading toward the table.

Sister Thelma noticing the maneuver, headed to another table with Rose in tow. She was a petite and pretty girl and Maribel was interested enough to see if she would be treated to 'the stare' but he just kept on talking to his leaders at the head table, not even glancing at Rose once.

She suddenly felt special, a feeling she had never encountered before with a man, and she liked it.

Sister Bertram made the welcoming remarks and Brian got

up to speak. The church hall was packed and he felt pleased that the church members had turned out to welcome him. The dinner actually made his job easier because tonight he could start putting faces to names and establish relationships.

She was sitting at the fourth table from the exit door. Her red dress was outstanding in a room of blacks and blues and greens—subconsciously she had dressed to stand out. It was both a come-on and a danger signal, he summed up.

While he headed for the small podium he wondered what he would say to this new flock of his. He whispered a prayer and asked God for guidance. It was not easy leading people with their various needs and personalities and their constant bids for attention from their spiritual adviser. He also had to navigate the fraught waters of single church sisters and create a balance where he was not seen as competition to his single church brothers.

"Good evening, saints of God." Brian cleared his throat. "Pastor Green sends greetings. I spoke to him just today and he reassured me that you are the best church he ever pastored and that I can expect many joys and spiritually uplifting times working in this corner of the vineyard."

They all smiled; some laughed.

"With the times we are living in I never expect anything to go smoothly, because if they are, then something is wrong. The church is expected to bear the banner of Jesus Christ to the world, and that is no easy task. It is not an easy task because we, who call ourselves Christians, are hampered by one fundamental issue, forgiveness. We are unable to forgive our neighbors and so God is unable to forgive us. Another issue is our blatant lack of trust in God. Without faith it's impossible to please God; without forgiveness, we ourselves are not forgiven. Where does that leave us?"

"Playing church," Sister Greenwood piped up at the front.

"Playing church," Brian smiled. "I don't mean to preach; I just want to say that I appreciate how difficult a job I may have taken on, but you can do your part among yourselves and we will have an even better church and correspondingly, a better society."

They all clapped, even her. She was looking at him fully now and he returned her look by adding, "I hope I can get to know each one of you in short order and that we can all be friends."

She looked away and he smiled out at the church hall. "I thank Sister Bertram and the Women's Ministries Department for such a thoughtful gesture."

He headed back to his seat, pleased that he had made an impact.

He is tall, Maribel thought dazedly, *and has the smooth, clipped, well-modulated voice of a cultured speaker.* The sermons could become erotic experiences if she didn't subject her thoughts to the Lord. She could just imagine him as a radio talk show host in the early hours of the morning, whispering any nonsense, and she would stay awake just to hear him with that smooth as honey voice.

"… Sister Maribel and the award-winning choir." Maribel jumped; she had so zoned out that she hadn't realized that Sis Bertram was at the podium and she was to sing next. She was so out of it she didn't remember what she was supposed to sing. She glanced across in panic at Cathy, who was standing up. She didn't know how she ended up at the podium with a mike in her hand but she felt the press of bodies behind her that was the choir as they gathered to back her up.

She wouldn't look at him, even though the podium was directly in front of the head table; Sister Bertram had set it up that way so that speakers and performers could face the head table.

Wise idea, Sister Bertram, she thought silently. "Lord forgive me for lusting after the pastor," she whispered before she started singing. Her nervousness passed after the first line of the song and she saw Sister Claudia rocking at her table in approval, so she continued in confidence, with the choir chipping in melodiously after her.

Brian closed his eyes to the very last note and joined the clapping when the choir and Sister Maribel left the podium. She had a gorgeous voice that alternated well between deep, high and melodious notes.

He was afraid to look at her after that; he concentrated on the rest of the program, responding to his leaders as they made any comments to him. He was a man and there was only so much a man could take after finding himself so attracted to a woman. He felt all shivery inside. It was as if angels sang when he saw her and the answer to his request for the Lord to find for him the best woman for a wife was answered.

He acknowledged within himself that love was not a first-sight situation; that was more like lust and the Bible spoke strongly against the lust of the flesh. He was not going to indulge any further in thoughts of Sister Maribel.

This was his fourth speech to himself after staring at her picture for three days like a lovesick puppy and now, having seen her in the flesh, he finally understood the dangers of sexual attraction. Having heard her sing he was teetering on the edge of an obsession that he had to nip in the bud and view her as just one of God's creatures that he should love with a brotherly love.

His convictions were still in place after the program finished and he mingled with the brethren. One Sister Carlene kept walking behind him, a big blue hat perched precariously on her head. Her mouth was practically drooling as she trailed him with an awestruck look on her face.

Sister Greenwood, whom he got to understand was the oldest woman in the church, kept introducing her granddaughters by telling him that they were of marriageable age.

"Oh Pastor…" He would turn around and she would have a granddaughter in tow, "this is Melissa, Barbara, Cassandra, Pandora … of marriageable age and childbearing hips."

He met the embarrassed looks of the various granddaughters with a kind smile and tried to put them at ease.

It took him half an hour to reach Maribel and her group.

She was laughing when he approached—a deep belly laugh. She could barely contain herself, and he found himself smiling in turn as her group gripped each other in mirth.

"Can I share in the joke?" he asked behind her.

She spun around and looked at him, the mirth still in her eyes. "Greg Norwood," she gestured to a young man standing beside a slim young woman who was clutching his hand, "his mother wanted to name him Habakkuk Malachi Norwood."

He grinned; she was obviously enjoying herself and it was impossible not to be affected by the sheer joy on her face.

"I will definitely remember your name then, Brother Norwood." He shook Greg's hand. "And I am guessing this is Sister Cathy?"

"Yes," Cathy said smiling at him, "we have counseling sessions with you starting next Tuesday."

"Oh yes." He looked at Maribel. "And you need no introduction. I was sitting and listening to your voice and I thought surely the Lord has bestowed upon you a wonderful gift."

"Thank you." Maribel suddenly felt bashful; she had been getting compliments all evening but none made her feel as if a great honor had been offered as the one she just received.

"I hear that you ladies in the Women's Ministry are doing great things in the community."

Maribel nodded. "I am a new member so I hear the same things too. I haven't started participating yet."

"Well, you have made a good start." He stared at her lips, and for a split second he forgot his name.

"So Pastor Edwards, what made you come to Jamaica?" He focused on Greg, who had asked the question, and gave some sort of answer; he couldn't remember what.

The tension between them had escalated; he could feel it and he knew her friends were picking up on it as well. He decided to leave. He wanted to ask for her number so that he could call her to start the courting ritual but he figured that he would be moving too fast, too soon, and he didn't want to scare her away.

Luckily, Sister Thelma rescued him as she practically shoved her daughter in his face. He watched as Maribel excused herself and left the church hall with her friends. The night for him lost a lot of its luster when she walked out in her red dress.

Chapter Five

"This is the third time I've caught you smiling fondly at your computer." Vivian popped her head around Maribel's door. "You haven't told me how the dinner went yesterday."

"Terrific, God is good." Maribel grinned at her friend.

Vivian sidled into the office and said hastily, "I would ask for the details but I just saw Mark heading this way—give me a file."

Maribel handed her a file, still smiling.

"When he passes he'll think we're consulting each other," Vivian said conspiratorially.

"The Fowler presentation went well," Maribel relaxed in her chair, "which was surprising, considering that I hardly slept last night. I was so tired when I left the dinner, and too keyed up to sleep."

"I hit the bed as soon as I reached home," Vivian said laughing. "My mother had to remove my shoes. I woke up this morning at four feeling as fresh as ever, though. So how did the song go?"

"Great, got compliments from nearly everyone, even the pastor."

"Ooh," Vivian opened her eyes wide, "is that a blush? Your ears are red."

Maribel put her hand in her head. "I think I have a huge crush. I have never, in my entire life, had a crush. Crushes are for wide-eyed, innocent teenagers but here I am with a gigantic crush on a pastor, of all the ironies in the world."

Vivian giggled. "That's not so bad, especially if it is reciprocated."

Maribel sighed.

"Is it?" Vivian piped up.

"Is it what?"

"You are prevaricating. Just tell me."

"Prevaricating." Maribel grabbed her dictionary.

"It means to beat about the bush, evade, hedge—it's on the notice board as the word of the day. Paul's mother is coming from England and I want to brush up on some big and impressive words."

"Then don't use big and impressive together," Maribel snorted. "I can't tell you the last time I looked at the notice board."

"Have it your way." Vivian threw up her hand in the air. "I am going to be singing a new song: Maribel's got a boyfriend nah-na-na-nah-na."

"Get out of here," Maribel said, laughing.

Mark stuck his head around the door when Vivian left. "Maribel, a minute in my office."

Maribel sighed and gathered some files together. The Fowler group had been satisfied with the work they got and were very impressed that it was done in such a short time. She had left the morning's presentation as pleased as punch, only to have Monster Mark hawk all the credit for himself.

She trudged after him, wishing that she had worn her most mousy work suit. Instead, even her below-the-knee brown suit, which was cut to her shape, suddenly felt too revealing.

"Lord, please be with me as I am about to face this monster. I mean man ... no offense meant God, but he must have the worst attitude of all your creatures."

Maribel stepped into Mark's office and glanced at him apprehensively. She looked around his spacious office, in which he had installed a mini golf play set. She was sure he didn't play but was just toadying up to rich clients.

"Maribel, I am very proud of how you handled the Fowler account." Mark cleared his throat.

Then why were you taking all the credit? Maribel thought silently.

"I was so impressed I decided to allow you to work on Hodges Construction. One of the biggest clients that we have; they employ over three thousand persons all over Jamaica."

"Is this in conjunction with the other companies that you have been giving me since you became my supervisor?"

Mark looked at her scornfully. "Why, don't think you can manage?"

"I am not going to work on any other major accounts along with Hodges'."

"Is that so?" Mark looked at her thoughtfully and swung in his chair. "Who is the boss here, Maribel?"

Maribel swallowed; he reminded her of how her father looked at her just before a beating. She thought that with adulthood she had gotten over this feeling of deep, dark fear whenever a man looked at her with cold contemplation, but today it was back in spades. She felt herself gearing up for flight when she heard Mark clear his throat. She looked up at him while she clutched the file folders so tightly that she could feel the papers being crushed by her vise-like grip.

"Okay, very well, at the next managing partners meeting I will mention that Hodges is too big an account to add to your work load."

"Thank you," Maribel said, relaxing her tight grip on the file folders.

"I deserve thanks, Maribel, in a more intimate way …" Mark changed his tone into a seductive purr.

Maribel stood up swiftly. "Is that all, sir?" She stressed the sir to breaking point, the exaggerated term of respect scornfully landing in the air between them.

"That's all." Mark looked at her measuredly, his eyes running swiftly over her body while she hurried out of his office.

Brian hurried into his office while checking the messages on his Blackberry. He had promised to visit two older members who were unable to attend church because of mobility problems, but he had to answer several urgent emails from his church family in Canada and also his parents. He was running behind schedule and Sister Thelma had almost mowed him down in the parking lot while he was parking his car.

"I am so happy I met up with you, Pastor." She was simpering behind him, "I just dropped off my daughter Rose to a seminar at the Pegasus. She's the managing director at her company, you know, just graduated magna cum laude from university with her masters."

"You don't say." Brian gestured for her to sit down in the chair opposite his desk. "I am going to check and send some email, Sister Thelma, so if you don't mind me being a bit distracted, you can continue the visit. If not, I have open vestry days on Tuesdays and Thursdays."

"I'll just sit with you a spell," Sister Thelma said, crossing her legs and getting comfortable. "I was just telling Rose how absolutely happy I was that she graduated with her MBA, and with such a high honor."

Brian grunted as he started typing the first email to his mother. His father, a retired judge, was having slight chest pains and his mother, the epitome of healthful living, was putting him on a rigid juice diet, which was causing the retired judge some angst.

He hurriedly typed that he missed them both. Being the first and only son meant that he was his mother's rock when his father was misbehaving, as she liked to fondly say— thankfully, Patsy had turned on the computer before he came in.

"I say, Pastor, do you realize how loose and morally deficient these young girls are these days, in church of all places?"

Brian grunted as he typed.

"I can barely look around in church without seeing miles of legs and bosoms. My Rose dresses conservatively and of course, with the utmost modesty."

"That's good for her," Brian mumbled as he sent off one mail and started another.

"I really hope your sermon this Sabbath is along the lines of modesty and purity, as befits the Christian faith."

"As a matter of fact it is." Brian looked up from his typing. "Not because of the short skirt wearing, though," he grinned at her, "but because its youth day."

"Please mention the sexual promiscuity and loose behavior, Pastor," Sister Thelma said gleefully. "I love it when these young people are shown the right and proper way."

Brian sighed; he didn't have time to set Sister Thelma straight about her judgmental attitude and to clarify that it was not only young people who were sexually promiscuous.

"I tell you, Pastor, if you preach that this Sabbath, I am going to drag Gunther to church kicking and screaming."

"Who is Gunther?" Brian asked interestedly.

"My son," she sighed. "Pastor, I don't know what to do with him. He is nineteen and claims he is taking a year off from school. He did sixth form and got all his A levels, so my husband Horace and I had big plans for him entering university. But alas, he holes himself up in his room, watching pornographic movies and listening to music that God's angels must shudder in distaste to hear. Recently he started growing and plaiting his hair. I told him that if he turns a Rasta in my house I am going to fumigate his room and throw out his things."

Brian could feel a counseling session coming on but he just did not have enough time for one without missing his previous commitments.

"Sister Thelma," he said as tactfully as possible, "I would really love to explore this problem with you some more so that we can both pray about it and look at practical ways to overcome this hurdle. Please ask Sister Patsy to schedule some time for you to see me next Tuesday."

"It's really the pornography I have a problem with," Sister Thelma said dejectedly, ignoring his hints for her to leave. "He doesn't even hide the abomination from his father or me anymore. He doesn't even bat an eyelid if I come into his room while he is watching them." She shuddered. "I am so thankful that Rose came out differently; my girl is the perfect child."

Brian shut down the computer and stood up. "Sister Thelma, walk with me. I am about to visit a shut-in member.

I will follow you to Sister Patsy's office while you schedule some time for next Tuesday."

She nodded and followed him out.

Chapter Six

Church was packed on Sabbath morning and Maribel was thankful that she got a seat under a fan. It was youth day, a day when the youth of the church ran the programs. The Youth Choir was singing today and she was quite happy that the senior choir was not required to be on duty—she didn't know if she had the energy to go through another nerve-racking performance so close to Thursday night's.

He was up there sitting on the platform, his handsome face looking freshly groomed. He looked strong and powerful in his tailored suit. It was no wonder some women were so attracted to pastors.

Tailored clothes tended to cover a multitude of dietary sins like love handles and beer bellies. A respectable suit gives such an aura of power to an otherwise ordinary male. Coupled with well-groomed hair and nails and maybe some perfume, they became gods in the eyes of their beholders.

She glanced at Pastor Edwards; he had on a pleasant smile

as his gaze raked over his congregation. It was not the well-fitting clothes or the smooth voice. It was just raw sexuality and magnetism that drew her.

Two qualities she had no business thinking about on the Lord's Day—or any other day, for that matter. Besides, his surface charm might just be hiding a terrible personality flaw, just because he was a pastor didn't mean he was good. Besides, she had slept with enough upstanding pillars of society to know that you can't judge a book by its cover.

She squeezed her eyes and tried to bury the past. She had asked for God's forgiveness but she could do nothing about the memories; they gathered in furor and tried to overcome her thoughts at the most inopportune moments.

There were days when faces seemed familiar and she was afraid that they were from her past. When men looked at her suggestively she wondered nervously if they had watched her on a porn video or seen a nude photo of her or had panted in heated lust on top of her in the back of a vehicle.

There was a gap in her life between God's forgiveness and her forgetfulness, and the stinging reminders of her past were still floating around the outside world; men were still lusting after her photos and watching her doing all types of perversions.

The organist and the pianist played a soothing note and Maribel dragged her mind back from the darkness of her past and tried to focus it on the present. Everybody knew that dwelling on the past was counter-productive; she schooled her features into an expression of peace and convinced her mind to stay right there.

"Great peace have they which focus on Christ, " she whispered to herself.

The pastor stood to speak, his voice falling over Maribel like the smoothest honey. "Brothers and Sisters in Christ, we are living and dwelling in a grand and awful time. It is a time when there are so many distractions in this world that we have a constant battle going on within and without.

"It is a time when good is scoffed at and the bad is celebrated; it is a time when our young people are torn between two loyalties, God and Satan, and have the added battle of sifting through the broken principles which our society has placed at odds with our value system.

"Our young women have skewed views about virginity and purity; they listen to what the world says: that it is okay to have sex before marriage. However, the Lord gave sex as a gift between two married people of the opposite sex."

Loud bellows of amen almost lifted the rafters of the church when the pastor said of the 'opposite sex.' It was a hot button topic that was sure to elicit a lot of self-righteous indignation and Maribel couldn't help the thought that he was pandering to the crowd.

She winced when his words about 'purity' and 'virginity' kept floating in the air; every word was like sandpaper against her flesh.

She could vaguely remember losing her virginity; she had run away from home and into the arms of a married fisherman. She tried to tune into what the pastor was saying but her mind kept returning to scenes from her past.

She had come home from school at exactly four o'clock— her father had worked out the timing of the route to the minute.

He would sit on the doorstep of their two-bedroom, part wood, part concrete house in Negril's West End. He would indolently sprawl on the tattered reclining chair on the veranda with a round alarm clock with two bells attached on the wooden railing and a thick leather belt resting beside it.

His sun-burnt skin, which had a fair yellowish hue in his

younger, better looking days, would be glistening with sweat. Maribel had thought that he was disappointed whenever she came home too early because she would thwart his much-anticipated 'clawting' of her.

He would declare, a feral gleam in his eye, before a beating, "I am going to clawt you with some lick y'see."

He usually gave her one minute to run before he ran after her with the leather belt he had taken the time to cure with pepper and salt. At times he would beat her until she couldn't scream anymore. He usually waited for weeks, until she was well again, to give her another beating.

The final evening when she decided not to take anymore of his brand of punishment, he was waiting on the veranda at the usual time. Maribel had just gotten her report card after the Christmas break. She had two C's, one in Geography and another in Social Studies. That would not go down well with her father. She had clutched the paper in her hand, not even considering that she could hide it from him. He usually got really angry when she kept any sort of secret from him and that would have warranted a "clawting." The last "clawting" had left her limping for days.

"Evening Dada." She had reached the step when the clock on the rail had trilled. He always set the time for four o'clock.

"Evening Gal." He got up and turned it off. "What's that?" He indicated the paper in her hand.

"My report." Her voice wobbled as she tremblingly held out the paper.

She closed her eyes tight and listened for the rustle of the paper and the creaking of the chair when he sat down in the recliner; she could even hear the slight wheezing in his breath when he inhaled. The silence dragged on and she tensed her body for a sudden blow. She opened her eyes slowly and there he was, the paper in his hand and his eyes closed.

"Er ... Dada."

"Yes Maribel."

"Er ... what do you think about the report?"

"I think I am going to kill you," he said, his eyes still closed. "I think I am going to just beat you to death until somebody call the police to come and get me."

He opened his bloodshot eyes and looked at her contemplatively. "I think I am going to watch your blood run over this yard and water my callaloo bed."

"But Dada, I got A's in Accounts and Mathematics."

He got up slowly, looking at her steadily. "Your mother was a harlot, a stinkin' whore. I took her when she was pregnant. I spent my money to school and feed her and she ran away. The ungrateful wretch that she spawned ran away too. Your mother left this place with a big belly tourist man and never looked back at you. I was supposed to raise you and make sure that you don't become like her."

Maribel froze as he advanced on her. The speech was usually the same, but the bloodlust in his eyes was different. He looked like he was really going to kill her.

"Two A's," he started yelling, "and two C's and two B's. What do you do at school all day? Run around with them renkin school boy?"

Maribel backed down the steps slowly as he grabbed the leather belt.

"I am going to give you a real clawting today, gal. Only God alone can stop me now."

Maribel had started to run by that time, and he had watched her as she ran through the gate. By the time she had reached the junction at the road she had seen a battered Toyota Corolla slowly navigating the potholes in the road. Her father had scampered after her and was breathing hard, his face twisted in angry bitterness.

The car had stopped and she had jumped in, not even looking to see who was driving.

"Drive," she had screamed to the startled driver and he had taken off, only stopping when he reached the main road.

"What happened?" the driver asked. He was a middle-aged man with tufts of hair growing in his ears. He had on a red polo shirt and a bandana around his neck. His eyes looked kind enough that she just melted in grief and poured out her heart to the man she later came to know as Murphy.

Murphy had put her up in his old fisherman shack and fed her. He understood her refusal to go back to school and her fear of her father. He also had a price for his assistance of her, and that had been her virginity. After she spent four months with Murphy his wife had come calling and Maribel was once more thrown on the street, with not even her school bag this time.

She tuned in to the sermon once more, just in time to hear the pastor remonstrating about the young men of today and their attitude toward young women and work. She could feel tears threatening as she recalled the way her father treated her.

She hadn't seen him since that day he ran her down with his cured leather belt in hand and suddenly realized that she hadn't asked the Lord to help her forgive him. She still resented him; the bitterness for forcing her into the world and into a lifestyle that she did not want was still strong, even nine years after her escape from home.

"And so my brothers and sisters, young men and women, keep yourselves pure, in deed, in thought, and in action—with God's help."

Maribel hung her head this time, quite distressed. So much for thinking there was even a chance with him; she wouldn't be able to live up to his lofty ideals of purity. She barely heard the closing song. She barely looked at the pastor when they shook hands at the door, even though his hands were warm and she had registered a faint tingling when she touched them.

"Sister Maribel," he had said warmly.

She was so relieved that the torturous sermon was over that she barely mumbled a greeting. She saw other people pushing to get closer to him, so she had enough time to move away, despite the fact that his fingers had tightened on hers to drag her back.

She had swerved quickly from the group that Cathy and Greg were standing in, jumped in her car and swiftly drove home, only to break down crying when she reached her apartment's parking lot.

She cried for the innocence she had lost, she cried for the fact that she would never regain it, and she cried that the one man with whom she could see herself living and growing old with would probably run away from her as far and as quickly as possible if he knew her past.

Chapter Seven

Brian rocked in his hammock, which was strategically hung between two palm trees in his backyard. The small yard was well landscaped, with diminutive June plum and mango trees and a water fountain feature. Obviously the owner was trying to create a tropical oasis in the middle of the city. His apartment complex was in the middle of New Kingston and yet when he came to his personal backyard he tended to forget that he was not in a country area.

He looked up through the palms at the small slice of sky that he could see from his vantage point and thought about Maribel. He had not liked the look on her face when she left church yesterday. She had a forlorn expression when he saw her in the receiving line. She had barely touched his hand in greeting and then she had rushed off, ignoring her friends and heading to her car like all the demons in hell were after her.

He wondered what had upset her so much. His mind

felt heavy with wondering what could be wrong with her. He had gotten her number from Cathy and as he swung in the hammock and clutched the phone to his chest, he kept rehearsing what he would say to her.

Should he just jump into the meat of the matter and enquire about the sad look she had yesterday? What should he do? He hadn't felt so twisted inside about a potential relationship since his middle school brush at romance with Tina Gonzalez.

The little Mexican minx had made him feel tongue tied and gauche—he was just twelve years old when he felt the first pangs of uncertain love blooming in his heart.

He felt the same way now, except that it was Maribel Contrell, the beautiful Jamaican girl, who had him tongue tied and out of sorts. He should probably ask her out to the church rally that he was invited to in St. Thomas. He would get a chance to speak to her and to get a handle on her personality during the drive to and from the venue.

He dialed her number and waited nervously for it to ring— from the moment that Cathy had handed him the number he had memorized it.

"Morning." Her voice sounded muffled, as if she was under a pillow.

"Hello Maribel." He paused. He could hear her inhaling sharply on the other line.

"Who is this?" she asked timidly, a hint of nervous anticipation in her voice.

He relaxed slightly and then realized how tense he was since he had dialed her number.

"This is Brian Edwards."

"Oh," she gasped, "Pastor Edwards ... I am ... could you hold a minute?" He heard rustling and then she came back on the line, "Pastor Edwards, er ..."

"I just called to find out how you are today." He closed

his eyes and pictured her in a red dress and that naked, vulnerable smile creeping across her face.

"I am fine," Maribel said chirpily, "good actually. I was just lazing around thanking God that I had no work to go to today."

"So you are free for the rest of the day?" he asked eagerly. She had already admitted that she was free and he was not going to give her a chance to backtrack.

"Yes ... well, I guess ... why?"

"I have a church rally in St. Thomas to attend at three o'clock and I was wondering if you can come?"

"Three o'clock..." She paused so long he looked at his knuckles and realized that he was gripping the telephone so tightly that the grooves on the bottom were digging into his hand.

"Ooookaaay," she dragged out the okay.

But that was fine with him; she had admitted that she was going to come with him to St. Thomas.

"That's good." He couldn't stop the smile from creeping into his voice. "Where should I pick you up?"

She gave him the address and directions.

"That's about five minutes from where I am at," he said to her smugly. "I'll be there at one."

"Okay ..." she was dragging out the okay in a breathless hiss this time and his heart picked up speed.

"Okay," he whispered, feeling elation wash over him.

"Step one, Lord," he said aloud when he hung up the phone. "Please guide me with the rest."

He had come for her at one o'clock on the dot; she had changed clothes so many times that her entire closet was strewn over her bed. She was going on a date with the pastor. She had pinched herself so many times and had stood looking in a daze at herself in the mirror, wondering if the sparkly-eyed girl staring at her was really the same girl who had been convinced yesterday that her attraction to Brian Edwards should just stay as unrequited affection, but here she was going to a church rally, the equivalent of a Christian date.

She really did not know much about Christian dating as she had never been out with a Christian before. She could remember having sex with several so-called Christian men but … she slammed the lid on the line her thoughts were taking and tried to concentrate on the wonderful present.

She had washed her hair and put in large curlers so that her hair would look fluffy when she took them out. Her favorite colors, red and pink, were vibrantly scattered in the ankle-length skirt she had put on. The fitted red blouse was modest enough to spare her blushes, yet fitted well enough to look feminine.

She was ready when she squirted a bit more of her favorite perfume onto her wrist. She had taken a deep breath, looked in the mirror and was sure that everyone in a one-mile radius would know how excited she was; she was just bursting with it.

She had stepped into his car, taken one look at him in his suit and was tongue-tied all the way out of Kingston. He hadn't seemed to be too talkative either, except for the speaking look of appreciation that he had raked over her body. He felt it too, she knew, and they were both trembling under the weight of their attraction.

He had Joe Rossi's version of *Bridge over Troubled Water* playing when he had looked at her and asked her if she liked the song. She nodded shyly and hummed to the song … *like a bridge over troubled water, I will lay me down …*

He had looked at her. "I am beginning to feel that way about you."

Maribel could barely look at him. She smiled and looked at the scenery that flashed by. Her body felt alive and tingling; her awareness of him was at its height—was this what it felt like to be in love? She grinned slowly when Aaron Neville's version of the Lord's Prayer came on.

"I like your taste in music." She looked at him sideways.

He smiled. "I am basically a gospel music-loving guy.

"Me too, I mean I am a gospel music-loving girl."

"Believe me Maribel," he said, "I have no doubts that you are a girl."

"You are making me blush."

He laughed. "You are making me lust but I won't hold that against you."

She smiled and squeezed her trembling hands together.

"I grew up in a small town in Toronto called Elora. Very clean and tranquil place, murderously cold in winter. My father, who was a judge at the time—he is now retired—used to regale us, my sisters and I, with stories about his days in Jamaica, especially in the winter months when we were snowed in—we called those days Jamaica Days. My mother would sit beside him, a wistful smile on her mouth, as they told us about back in the days when they were in Jamaica.

"My father grew up in Negril, Westmoreland and my mother grew up in Montego Bay. They actually met at a church rally."

Maribel gasped, her mind running—Negril. She dearly wished that the name of that town hadn't come up to put a blight on her day.

"So, how many sisters do you have?" she hastily asked, maybe she could get him to talk about his family and ignore hers. A fatalistic voice in her head snorted, *Yeah, right.*

"Just three," Brian laughed, "twins born one year after me, and our baby sister, who my mother still refers to as an unexpected gift. She was conceived in Jamaica when my parents came back here for their second honeymoon. She's just turned sixteen."

"So is this your first time in Jamaica?" Maribel turned to look at him and then his clean square fingers on the steering wheel.

"Oh no," Brian looked at her, aghast. "Don't you realize that I am a partial yard man?" he said, unsuccessfully trying to speak the Jamaican dialect.

Maribel laughed.

"Actually, I used to come here every summer when my grandparents were alive. I spent all my vacations in Negril up until I started college. My grandfather was a teacher and my grandmother a fat, happy housewife who was puzzled that all her efforts at trying to fatten her very slim husband came to naught. I think she fed him too much fatty foods and it finally took a toll on his heart. After several warnings from his doctor, warnings he ignored because he was so addicted to his wife's cooking, his pressure went up and his heart went out."

Maribel choked on a laugh. "You are not serious."

"Oh yes," Brian glanced at her. "My grandmother was a lavish butter and sugar user. I can remember my mother, who is a health nut, feverishly praying at her bedside for our health before we left for Jamaica. She knew how my grandmother was, but my father insisted that his children should be in touch with their Jamaican heritage, so we had to come here every summer. Ironically, food was not the reason Grandmamma died."

"How did she die?"

"She was hit by a car on her way from the market. I mourned

her loss greatly, I must tell you. She was instrumental in me being a pastor."

"She was?" Maribel asked, interested to know why he chose to take on such a responsibility.

"She used to insist that I prepare and preach sermons to her on the veranda of her home in Negril. She would call over other family members and friends and they would listen as I expounded on the Word. I guess it was her way of ensuring that I read the Bible and it was also a source of entertainment for her. I really loved doing it and I guess my basic love for people ensured my career path."

Maribel grinned, "I must remember that if ever I marry, have children and want one or two of them to choose a career in the church."

He slowed down and waited behind a vehicle that was turning onto a side road. "Something tells me that you will marry and have children. It is surprising that you are still single. At the risk of sounding clichéd, why are you still wandering around this world unattached?"

"I am waiting for …"

"The right man," he finished for her and laughed. "How old are you, Maribel?"

"Twenty-five."

He nodded and smiled.

"What?" Maribel asked, laughing. "What does that smile mean?"

"It means nothing. I can't explain how happy I am to be in Jamaica this year at this time … with you."

Maribel felt her heart pounding faster after that declaration.

"So why did you look so sad yesterday?"

"Ah … nothing."

"Mmmmm," Brian said disbelievingly and waited for her to talk.

"Well … " Maribel swallowed, thinking how to give him a sanitized version of how her life had been, "I was thinking about my childhood and I got a bit misty-eyed."

"What about your childhood made you misty-eyed?"

"My mother ran away from home when I was thirteen with a German guy, my sister ran away shortly after that with a fisherman and then my father became abusive to the lone female left in his radius."

"Oh," Brian said, "when I saw you at first, I would have guessed that you were a pampered girl living in a two-parent family with a doting father and possibly a mother who brags to all and sundry about you."

Maribel sighed, "Looks can be deceiving, Pastor Edwards."

Brian laughed, "Don't Pastor Edwards me, Sister Contrell." He glanced at her. "Call me Brian."

"Well Brian, people are not always all they seem to be."

"That is a loaded statement that I want to pursue with you later." Brian nodded. "So where in Jamaica were you living before Kingston?"

Maribel glanced at him. He was driving along asking questions which on the surface were so simple, but to her were such a big part of the barriers that she had placed around herself to protect her new identity and to forget about the past. Here he was tearing through her barriers and doing so quite cheerfully.

"Maribel?" He glanced over at her tense expression. "Is it top secret?"

"Oh … no … I was born in Westmoreland. Grew up in Negril."

"Negril?" Brian glanced at her. "You didn't say a word when I was telling you about my grandmamma. Do you know I still have family there? Maybe one day you and I can take a drive down there."

"No!" Maribel shouted. She could feel herself getting very agitated at the mention of such an idea. She would not be going back to Negril even if her life depended on it.

Brian looked at the car clock; it was saying two o'clock—they would still reach St. Thomas on time.

He looked over at the sea, which appeared a bit grey; the day was rapidly becoming overcast. "Maribel, I did not mean to pry. I just wanted to get to know you better."

Maribel whimpered, almost hugging the door. *Pull yourself together, Maribel,* she kept telling herself, *it's not as if he is going to hire a private investigator and delve into your life. He's just being friendly.*

"I am sorry." Her voice was hoarse; she cleared her throat. "I am sorry, I just get really paranoid when I think of Negril. You see, I ran away from home at sixteen. I was taken in by strangers and … " she squeezed her eyes tight. "I just hate to think of it."

"It's okay." Brian shifted in his seat and thought about hugging her but warning signals went off in his head.

He couldn't handle hugging Maribel; this was just too clichéd a situation for him to get in trouble. Single pastor hugging single, extremely attractive church sister in the middle of a deserted stretch of road would mean trouble. He settled for patting her hand and then quickly drew it away.

"Okay, here's the deal." He grinned at her. Her eyes were glassy; they looked so vulnerable and appealing. He looked at her trembling lower lip and completely forgot what he was about to say.

"The deal?" Maribel prompted him.

"Oh yes." He straightened in his seat, wishing he could arrange his pants properly; probably this drive was not such a good idea after all. "I think we should forget about Negril; just tell me about happy things. How is that?"

Maribel looked at him thoughtfully. "Okay, I can manage that."

"Good, then let's go to that rally and then we can indulge ourselves with huge ice cream cones. Are you game?"

"Oh yes," Maribel laughed, happy that Negril was out of the discussion. She vowed never to bring it up again and hoped that he would forget it too.

Chapter Eight

"**M**aribel." Christa, the receptionist, peered through Maribel's door as she sat staring at the Hodges Construction file bemusedly.

They had reached the rally on time and everyone thought they had been a couple. She smiled as a little bubble of joy rose to the surface of her thoughts; they had actually called her Sister Edwards. She scrawled Maribel Contrell Edwards on the file, right beside where she had written Mrs. Brian Edwards in stylized writing, and then glanced up vaguely at the door.

Christa was staring at her, smiling; in her hands was a bouquet of red roses. "This was delivered for you."

Maribel's eyes lit up. "I have never gotten roses delivered to me before."

Christa sniffed the full blood-red petals once more and handed them over to Maribel. "We read the card in the reception area before I carried it to you."

"Who's we?" Maribel asked, taking the flowers from Christa and grabbing eagerly at the card, which was attached to the beautiful glazed vase by a string.

"All of us who were in the front at the time," Christa said, with no apparent shame in her voice at her snooping.

Maribel read the note, "If I speak in the tongues of men and of angels, but have not love, I am only a resounding gong or a clanging cymbal. Signed, BE."

"Now my question is," Christa said, peering once more at the card, "who is BE?"

Maribel felt a strange flutter in the region of her heart as she clutched the card to her chest. "Be gone, Christa," she shooed Christa out of the office.

Christa shuffled out, grumbling, "Why would a bee send you a Bible verse?"

"Because he is absolutely romantic and wonderful ..." Maribel took the flowers and placed them in the middle of her crammed desk. Now how was she supposed to get any work done with the gentle aroma of the roses reminding her that BE was on a mission to woo her?

Maribel Contrell, former prostitute, who had all but given up on romance, was now being courted. She had to stop herself several times from grinning goofily at the payroll for Hodges Construction. She caressed the file tenderly as her mind wandered to marital thoughts. It was so romantic of Brian to send her that Bible love chapter quote from I Corinthians 13.

"I came as soon as I heard," Vivian exclaimed breathlessly from the door.

Maribel grinned, "Can you imagine the audacity of the receptionist to read my note?"

Vivian snorted and snatched it up herself. "If I speak in the tongues of men ... " she grinned, "now who could BE be?"

"Him," Maribel said dreamily.

"I know," Vivian said. "I didn't know things were getting serious."

"Well …" Maribel's voice trailed away as her phone rang. She glanced at the number on the display and scowled: internal call, Monster Mark.

"Hello," she answered the call primly.

"Maribel," Mark said, his voice sounding hostile, "I need to see you in my office now."

"Yes sir." Maribel placed the phone in the cradle and stuck her tongue out at it.

"Got to go, Viv, the Monster demands my presence."

Vivian got up. "See you at lunch."

Maribel checked her green skirt suit and sighed. There was nothing she could do about her shape—short of wearing a bag to work, she would always feel a little sensitive where Mark was concerned.

She walked into his office after a brief knock and was surprised to see him standing at the window with his back to her.

"Sir?" she enquired of him formally.

He glanced at her, a smirk on his face, "You know, Maribel, I am pleased to see that my instincts about you were right."

"What are you talking about?" Maribel demanded.

"Well … " His eyes ran up and down her body and he gave a suggestive lick of his lips, "I always knew you were a bit on the wild side."

He had never blatantly harassed her like this and Maribel felt heat engulf her face in anger. "Listen, I am going to report you to Human Resources. I don't care if it's your word against mine, you have crossed the line."

"So have you." He held up a picture in his hand of two nude women in a suggestive pose. Their eyes were turned up in a come-hither look as they both bent over a huge lollipop. Their tongues were caressing the sweet; one had a riding crop at her feet and the other had her finger crooked in a come-hither gesture. The one with the riding crop was her. She did not have on a stitch of clothing and her blonde wig was piled high on her head. All of her features could be seen.

"This is a conservative firm, dear Maribel, and I cannot allow you to go around taking sexually explicit photos to embarrass us."

Maribel's heart rate speeded up; she felt lightheaded and faint. "I was very young when I took that photo."

Mark laughed and sat down in is chair. "I don't mind the picture, you understand." His long fingers caressed her features on the photo and he glanced up at her. "I can keep this very quiet. Nobody else has to know about it."

The hairs on Maribel's neck stood up and she groped around and sank into one of two chairs in front of his desk. She knew without a doubt that he had her right where he wanted her.

She thought about the mortgage on her just-purchased apartment and cringed. If she didn't find another job in, say, six months she wouldn't be able to pay her bills, and she might have to go back on the streets—she needed this job.

She knew she was panicking. She felt hot and itchy in her suit and tears were welling up in her eyes.

Lord Jesus, why me? Why does my past have to rear its ugly head now? Why Lord?

"I am not going to sleep with you," Maribel croaked out, recoiling from the leer in Mark's eyes.

"I don't require you to be sleeping," Mark said lasciviously. "I want you awake and functioning when I strip your clothes and take you, preferably on this desk after work. I would say tonight but I promised my wife to do something for her.

I could wriggle out of it but I am going to be very busy for many nights to come with you."

"No Mark. I won't be doing anything with you." She thought frantically, *How am I going to get myself out of this mess?* "I am not going to stoop to your blackmail."

"I don't want you stooping—at least, not yet," Mark had a glazed look of lust in his eyes. "I want you bent over."

"Stop it," Maribel yelled, getting up and heading to the door. "Where did you get that picture anyway?" Her hands were trembling.

"I had to pay very good money to a friend of mine who saw you at the office the other day and remarked how alike you were to an old nude pinup he had."

Maribel cringed. "I am not going to have sex with you, Mark; do your worst."

Mark walked up to her and took her hand from the door. He whispered in her ear, "You smell so good." He ran his fingers along her arms. "If I hadn't promised Cindy to drop off those damn pills for her mother, you and I could start what we were meant to do tonight."

His feather-light touches made Maribel's skin crawl, and she shuddered in distaste at his heavy breathing as he angled his body closer to hers.

He laughed softly. "See, I am making you shiver with longing already. All this cold attitude toward me was an act, wasn't it?"

Maribel shrugged away from him, her thoughts in a jumble. Look how happy she was this morning when she received the flowers, and now she was facing the most abhorrent situation that could happen to a woman in the workplace.

An insidious voice was telling her to just have sex with him; after all, she used to do it with strangers in the street and at the back of buildings. The voice sneered at her and had the gravelly texture of her father's drawl.

The other voice, which was not as loud but just as insistent, was telling her to trust God.

Trust him Maribel; he knows your past; he forgave you; don't go back; trust him. Tears sprang to her eyes and she jumped when Mark's phone rang. So tightly had she withdrawn inside herself that she hadn't noticed that Mark had loosened his tie and started to unbutton his shirt after locking the door.

What was he thinking? she thought in a panic. Did he think she would have sex with him between lunch and coffee break?

He looked at the ringing phone murderously and then back at her.

"What!" he answered in a growl. "Okay, I'll get it now." His voice gentled and took on a wheedling tone. He was probably talking to one of the partners, Maribel thought as she looked at his handsome profile and thought that he was evil personified.

"I've got to go to a meeting with one of the partners." He looked at Maribel coldly. "I expect you to do as I say, Maribel, or you are out of here, and don't expect any references either."

Maribel grabbed the door and could barely open the lock; she left the office, stumbling through the passageway, and was very grateful to sit in her own chair.

She remembered so clearly the day she took that picture with Felicia. They had just met; Murphy's wife had ignominiously thrown her out of the cottage with nothing. She had walked aimlessly through Negril, contemplating whether she should go back home and have her father kill her; it would take care of her having to commit suicide.

She had felt so down and hungry with no one to turn to;

her father had ensured that she had no friends. Even the neighbors in the district had been afraid to show her kindness because they knew that she would pay for it if her father ever found out.

So alone in the world was she that she couldn't even call a family member. The members of her mother's family were somewhere in Clarendon; they had abandoned her mother when she had gotten pregnant in third form in high school. Her mother had turned to her father, an older man who had expressed interest in her and was willing to take her with the pregnancy, and had moved her to Negril, away from her family.

She knew next to nothing about her father's family, but if they were anything like him she stood a better chance on the streets. She wandered to a food court in a popular mall and sat down, watching tourists and locals alike enjoying themselves and eating.

Her belly growled at the torturous sights before her and she had looked longingly as people chewed their foods, their jaws working in a torturous rhythm before they swallowed.

After half an hour of torture, a girl who looked about her age had sat down beside her and handed her a patty.

"Thanks." Maribel had looked at her curiously; she was half Indian with a long curly ponytail reaching her waist. She had an almost elfin look and had grinned at her sheepishly. "I was watching you when you came in. I knew you were hungry but I thought you were waiting for someone. My name is Felicia, by the way."

She spoke with a slight Eastern Caribbean accent and Maribel had warmed up to her instantly. She had poured out her story to Felicia, who had listened sympathetically and then replied that she was a runaway too. However, she had money because she worked for it.

How did she work for it?

She took nude pictures for tourists who liked the kinky stuff, but she was working now with an American guy who sold pictures to magazines. Of course the pay was good, she had replied to Maribel's halting queries.

Maribel's joy at finding something to do and a decent place to sleep that night had resulted in her taking several suggestive pictures for the photographer and his partner. They had gotten her drunk that evening and she barely remembered the poses and sexual acts she had engaged in. She just remembered that the morning after they had kicked Felicia out of the beachside house, accusing her of stealing money. Not wanting to lose her only friend, Maribel had followed.

Both of them had started working on the streets after that, but only for a year. Days were spent catching up on sleep in a one-room they both rented from a man with a beer belly; they had taken turns giving sex in exchange for rent. They nicknamed him Piglet because of his pink florid features and broad flat face. Felicia had declared, almost from the first, that absolutely nobody should know their real names and so they had become Peaches and Cream.

Maribel blinked rapidly at her computer screen; her past was never going to let her go. What were the odds, that of all the pictures in the world, Mark's friend should have that picture with her in it?

She hadn't even known that the photographers had used them. She just remembered an overwhelming smell of marijuana in the house by the beachside and the clicking sound of camera shutters as the men, one black and one white, had yelled out instructions. They had plied her with drinks to make her giggle and to loosen her up, they had said. The come-hither look in her eyes was merely as a result of a drugged-up high.

Her life was now on a slippery bend careening out of control; where was God in all of this? Why couldn't He just cause all the photos, videos and memories of her life to just be obliterated from the face of the earth?

What about Brian? She sighed as she looked on the vase with roses. He didn't deserve her kind of life entangling with his.

"Oh Maribel."

She looked up wearily. Charisa was at the door. "Here is another delivery from BE; I checked."

Maribel took the gift box from her and read the note. Her heart felt heavy in her chest and she felt an overwhelming urge to cry. 'If I have the gift of prophecy and can fathom all mysteries and all knowledge and if I have faith that can move mountains but have not love I am nothing.'

Charisa smiled as she headed for the door. "I think this is so romantic."

Maribel sniffed, "Close the door on your way out, please." She listened as the door clicked and put her head on the Hodges Construction file and had a good bawl.

Chapter Nine

"**H**ey Brian." Maribel tried to inject some brightness in her voice. "Thanks for the flowers and the chocolate that you sent today. I was trying to get through to you but I couldn't."

Brian chuckled down the phone line. "I was tied up in a very intense meeting at the church headquarters. So did you like them?"

"I loved them. I loved the notes too."

"First Corinthians thirteen has thirteen verses," Brian reminded her.

"Don't tell me you are going to send a gift for each verse?"

"I am not telling you," Brian murmured. "Say Maribel, are you tired?"

"Not really," Maribel said. "I had a tough day today but I am pretty keyed up."

"Would you like to walk with me up Widcombe Heights? I am itching to go outdoors and work up a sweat."

"Sure," Maribel said brightly. That sounded like a good

idea to her; at least she could forget the foolishness that took place at the office today instead of staying home and stewing about it.

Should she or shouldn't she have sex with Mark? The question was bouncing off her brain as she sat staring sightlessly at her television. Blackmail had a way of mushrooming out of control, she knew; the blackmailer was never satisfied until they sucked you dry and left you with nothing, and the irony was that despite the blackmail and hush-hush money or favors, somebody always found out and broadcast your secret to the world.

She cringed to think of all the people at work seeing that picture or knowing that was the reason for her dismissal; she could almost see them lining up to condemn her, and where would she find another accounting job after discreet little hints were dropped in certain ears about her secret life as a nude model? Nobody would take her seriously and her protestations of the picture belonging to a past life would dig up a whole new line of questioning about her past.

She dragged on her track bottoms and found a matching top that was not too clingy but still looked decent.

Brian picked her up at the gate and she instantly felt light-hearted. All her woes seemed to melt when she saw his warm brown eyes and his chiseled, handsome features, which had become so dear to her in such a short period of time—if he only knew what she was now facing and the questions that were floating around in her head.

Brian handed her a gift bag when she sat in the car. Maribel sighed, "You are spoiling me."

Brian laughed. "Open it."

She opened the bag and it was a bottle of water. On the water hung a card. She read aloud, "If I give all I possess to the poor and surrender my body to the flames but have not love I gain nothing."

"I thought about putting your name inside that text. If I give all I possess to the poor and surrender my body to the flames but have not Maribel I gain nothing."

Tears came to Maribel's eyes. "I don't think I am worth it, Brian."

"I do," Brian said sincerity in his voice. "Wait until you get the next gift."

"So this gift was just to make sure that I am well hydrated on our walk."

"Yes ma'am." He glanced at her. "When you laugh like that you look so innocent and vulnerable I feel like protecting you from the cares of this life."

Maribel inhaled sharply. "Brian ... er ... I am not as innocent as I seem."

"It is rare for people to be as innocent as they seem," Brian said dryly. "It's just that you appear that way."

"Well ..." Maribel bit her lip, "I am far from innocent."

Brian shrugged. "That's a concept we will have to explore on our walk."

He parked the car and they stretched on the roadside. "My helper told me about this place," Brian said, a smug smile on his face. "I can see why she suggested it."

"It's a tough hill," Maribel said, glancing at him. "Are you sure you are up to it?"

"I have Jamaican genes," Brian snorted. "Is it not a fact that there is some superhuman athletic gene that was specially given to Jamaicans by God?"

Maribel laughed. "I don't know about that, unless hard work and wanting something bad enough is unique to Jamaicans."

"Well let's see what you have," Brian said, briskly walking before her. Maribel checked out his firm, well-shaped butt in his blue tracksuit and almost got caught licking her lips.

"Come on, Miss Jamaica," Brian said sternly, "let's see you in action."

Maribel ran beside him and laughed.

"Okay, Mademoiselle Maribel," Brian said leeringly, "what is this insinuation that you are a debauched female on the loose?"

Maribel looked at him solemnly. "I am just saying that I am not as innocent as I seem."

"Okay," Brian looked thoughtful, "so you have had a boyfriend before, is that it? A subtle warning to me that you are not a virgin and I shouldn't get my pastorly hopes up?"

"Well … " Maribel walked a bit faster ahead of him and thought quickly, *A boyfriend—now that was an understatement if ever there was one.* Her past sexual partners probably ranked in the high three figures. *Just tell him and get it over with,* the little voice urged her. *Stop it now; let him deal with it now.*

But he won't talk to you again, another voice reasoned with her. *He will probably look at you as if you have leprosy after this. He'd probably spit in the road when he sees you coming and cross to the other side.*

Brian stopped in front of her, forcing her to halt and look into his eyes; they were a rich, chocolate-brown; a lighter brown ring circled his irises. It was a feature she would probably have missed if she weren't this close. She could actually feel the warmth from his body as she stood as still as possible. Other walkers walked around them as they stood still, staring into each other's eyes.

"It doesn't matter," Brian said to her finally. "Not to make you feel bad, but I have never been with anyone. I firmly believe that sex should be for marriage; in that regard I am very much a by-the-book pastor."

Maribel nodded, her heart racing out of control.

"When you are ready, you can tell me about your past." He pushed a lock of hair from her brow and looked at her lips hard. "Suddenly I am very in need of some steam release." His voice was husky. "Let's walk and talk about work."

Maribel exhaled when he stepped away and tried hard to get some much-needed air into her lungs. "Your work, not mine," she said breathlessly. "I had the roughest day on record."

"I am sorry to hear that." Brian smiled at her. "My day was interesting. I visited a sick church sister today; I had no idea that in modern times people still wore mop caps. You know, those frilly, fluffy caps that Little Red Riding Hood's grandmother used to wear."

"Oh, I know Little Red Riding Hood's grandmother," Maribel nodded sarcastically, "but only because I work for the wolf that ate her."

Brian laughed. "Well, this sister had on one of those hats. She's diabetic, so her overworked daughter watches everything she eats. While we were speaking and her daughter went elsewhere, she took out a chocolate bar from under the mop cap and said to me conspiratorially, 'Parson, I've got to have a little sweetness in my life.'

"I nodded, feeling a little wary of being part of a conspiracy, but then she took out another one and then another one. By the time I had gotten up I was thinking that she had a candy shop in her head."

Maribel stopped and laughed at the side of the road. "I haven't laughed like this in ages. Maybe you should switch jobs with me."

Her work-related problem was waiting for her in the

lobby the next day with a smirk on his face. He held up a package in his hand. A familiar card was hanging from it. He sneered at her. "For Maribel," he read from the note. "Love is patient, love is kind, it does not envy, it does not boast, it is not proud."

"How quaint Maribel," he mocked. "Have an admirer, huh? Let's see what's in here." He peered into the paper bag. "Bagels, chocolate-coated bagels."

"That's mean," Christa, who had snuck behind the receptionist desk while Mark was sneering and snorting, said to him. "You shouldn't have looked into her delivery like that."

"I saw you look in there first," Mark said to Christa impatiently.

"That's because I am a woman. I can snoop."

Maribel could feel a scream making its way from the bottom of her belly, heading to her lips, when Vivian stepped through the door and bumped into her.

"Glorious morning, everyone." She took in the scene in the lobby and stood beside Maribel, her smile fading.

Mark scowled at them; they were all looking at him as if he had lost his senses. He dropped the package on the receptionist desk and growled, "Maribel, my office, now."

Maribel sniffed. "Yes sir," she said in a clipped tone.

"If I never," Vivian was whispering to her, "he is one arrogant pig."

"I've got something to tell you," Maribel said to Vivian as she collected her latest gift from Brian.

"Tell on," Vivian said gleefully as they stepped into Maribel's office. Vivian peeped into the bag and took out a bagel as Maribel placed her briefcase and handbag on the desk. "It says here that love is kind," she held up the note, "so share with your starving colleague."

"Viv," Maribel said seriously, sitting down hard in her chair, "Mark found a nude photo of me and is trying to blackmail me to sleep with him."

Vivian was about to bite into the bagel and looked at Maribel wide eyed. "Run that by me again."

"You heard me," Maribel said seriously.

"Where?" Vivian asked, putting down the bagel on a napkin gingerly.

"Where what?" Maribel asked impatiently.

"Where would Mark get a picture of you in the nude?"

"Long story," Maribel said, panicking. "He's calling me in his office to rub in that he has the upper hand. I prayed about the situation last night and there is no way I am going to have sex with that creep. The Lord reminded me that he will take care of me through thick and thin."

"Whew," Vivian exhaled, "that's a relief to know. Never sleep with a married creep who is blackmailing you."

"I am just at a loss as to what to do," Maribel said, looking pained. "I tossed and turned last night searching for ways that I can avoid this."

Vivian started rustling in her bag. "I had this urge to bring this to work today."

Maribel stood up. "What's that?"

"It's a tape recorder," Vivian said smugly. "This should do great."

"Okay," Maribel nodded, "what do I do?"

"Well," Vivian whispered, leaning toward Maribel, "the problem with this scenario is that Mark the blackmailer has recently married—the daughter of this company's president."

Maribel's eyes lit up. "You lie."

Vivian nodded. "Unlike you, I listen to the grapevine. Recently married to the boss's daughter and is trying to blackmail you. Listen, this might not be an original idea, but my advice to you is to record him. Play it back to him. If he is still stubborn, send it to his father-in-law or wife and see how fast the idiot backtracks."

"I could kiss you," Maribel said, taking the slim tape recorder and slipping it into her jacket pocket.

"Well … the grapevine has switched their assessment that you are a lesbian since you started receiving those presents, so kissing me may muddy the waters a bit."

"Viv …" Tears came to Maribel's eyes. "Thank you, you didn't hesitate to help, and that joke is not funny."

Vivian snorted. "I want you to stop panicking and to nip this bullying in the bud. No woman deserves this kind of work-related harassment."

Maribel headed to Mark's office with a lighter and more determined step than she had ever taken. She walked into the office and looked at the mini golf course in disdain.

He was seated behind his desk. "I asked you to come to my office ten minutes ago; what are you playing at?"

"I had to settle in for the day, Mark." She lowered her voice into a husky drawl, a skill that she had perfected from back in the days when she used to hang over the front door of cars in the night. She strolled over to his desk and bent over slightly taking care that the tape recorder wouldn't fall out.

"Wow, Maribel." His cold eyes softened. "I knew this holier-than-thou-attitude would not last. You want me, don't you?"

"Yes Mark," Maribel drawled, "I want you." *To lose your job and leave this company,* she added silently to herself.

"Lock the door Maribel," Mark said, getting to his feet.

Maribel drew back a bit from the desk as he advanced toward her. "I stay up at nights dreaming about you." He stood in front of her. "Dreaming about us on my desk."

"You don't say," Maribel murmured, hoping that the

recorder was picking up his breathy, rasping voice.

"Is it too early for us to ditch work and go to a hotel for the day? I have to be back here by three for a meeting with the bosses. Damn these infernal meetings."

Maribel murmured, commiserating. "What about your wife? What will she say about us?"

"She won't know," Mark said to Maribel sharply. "What I am getting at home is nowhere near enough to satisfy me."

"I see." Maribel stepped back. He was practically pressing into her; she could smell the coffee scent on his breath.

"Where are you going?" Mark asked her sharply.

Maribel turned back and flashed him a seductive smile. "To the door. Do you have any more copies of that picture?"

"Oh no," Mark said grinning. "I had to convince Pete it wasn't you for him to part with it. I paid him a lot of money for it."

Maribel turned back from the door and said coldly, "Give it to me."

"Hell no." Mark held up his hand. "Are you crazy?"

Maribel took out the recorder from her jacket pocket and pressed rewind. *I stay up nights dreaming about you* wafted in the air in the office.

"Give me the picture, I won't send this to your wife and your father-in-law, and we forget that you ever had the nerve to try to bribe me with that photo."

"You bitch," Mark bit out as he headed toward Maribel.

"Take one step further and I will not only send this to your wife but charge you with assault as well."

Mark stopped in his tracks, looking stunned.

"If you even look at me in any way inappropriate again, I will create such a stink about it that you will have trouble. Are you understanding me?"

Mark nodded, his shoulders slumping. "The picture is in

here." He unlocked a drawer and pulled it out.

"Now light it afire," Maribel said, gritting her teeth.

"How do I know that you will destroy that tape?" Mark bit out, his jaw clenched tightly.

"I am no blackmailer," Maribel growled. "I was reduced to this because of your assumptions that I would be scared enough to have sex with you and allow you to trample on my dignity. I won't allow it."

"You are no saint, Maribel," Mark said, lighting the paper afire. "Good girls don't pose so suggestively."

"Have you made copies?" Maribel asked him coldly.

"Hell no," Mark said huffily, "I wouldn't want my wife to find it; now destroy that tape."

Maribel took out the little cassette and dragged out the strip and dropped it on the floor.

"Have a blessed day, sir," she said, reaching for the door and dragging it open, then she made sure that her voice carried because she saw Annette from Human Resources coming. "And if you ever call me in your office for anything that is not work related I am going to take you to court for sexual harassment. Do you understand me?"

Mark's humble 'yes' was clearly heard by Annette and she paused, looking at Maribel wide-eyed.

Chapter Ten

Maribel was so ecstatic that she had nipped the problem of Mark in the bud that she had flung her briefcase on her settee as soon as she stepped into her apartment and started playing her favorite Tina Turner CD.

She always played it when she was in a good mood; she had hummed it all day at lunch when she and Vivian had met to crow over her triumph. She ran into her room for her brush and turned up the stereo high; at the top of her lungs she belted out the words, closing her eyes and thinking of Brian's handsome face. Maybe they could make it if he didn't find out about her past—she was in the mood to be delusional.

She began to strip and sing in her heels, hiking up her work skirt; in a parody of Tina's voice she sang *River Deep Mountain High*.

She barely registered when the phone's shrill ring interrupted her first verse.

Dang. She frowned as she picked up the phone.

"Hello," she yelled down the phone line. "I can't hear you." She didn't pretend to decipher whose voice was on the phone as her song droned on.

"Maribel," Brian chuckled, "I can see I have called at a bad time."

"No, oh no," Maribel turned down the stereo, "I get a little carried away when I sing this song and I was just at the sweetest verse."

"Sing it for me," Brian said huskily.

"Now?" Maribel squealed.

"Of course; give me a slice of Maribel when her hair is down and she is at her most relaxed."

"Well … " Maribel hesitated; she didn't want him to think she was crazy.

"Can I see you now?" Brian asked urgently.

"Now?" Maribel asked anxiously. "But you just asked me to sing the second verse."

"I want to see you singing it," Brian said decisively, "and I have something for you."

"Damn … I mean … Darn … I am not quite dressed for visitors." She snatched up the cordless phone and grabbed her briefcase from the settee. Luckily, her helper had been in just yesterday so her two-bedroom apartment looked neat.

"Are you finished being frantic?" Brian asked, a smile in his voice.

"Yes …" Maribel skated to her room, threw the briefcase on her bed, and buttoned up her blouse.

"Well, I am at your door." Brian murmured.

"That's so … what do you mean at my door? You mean at my apartment door?" Maribel ran a comb through her hair and ran into the bathroom to wash her face.

"At your gate," Brian responded. "The security is going to

call you now to ask for permission to let me in."

"Okay." Maribel hung up the phone and finished washing her face.

By the time the security had let in Brian and she heard her doorbell ringing, her heart was pounding a mile a minute, as if she had just completed a quarter-mile run.

She opened the door and breathlessly looked at him. He was casually dressed in black jeans and a black t-shirt.

He stared back at her in silence.

"Aren't you going to ask me if I am not going to let you in?" Maribel asked, babbling. "My hand feels frozen on the door."

Brian laughed and stepped by her when she stepped away; he had a paper bag in his hand. He handed it to her when he went into her living room.

She took it from him and saw the card hanging from it. "This smells nice." She looked in the bag. It was filled with containers.

"Dinner." Brian stood with his hands in his pockets.

"Make yourself at home," Maribel belatedly said. She looked at the card and read silently. 'Love is not rude, it is not self-seeking, it is not easily angered, it keeps no record of wrongs.'

She sighed and said out loud, "If only this was true for us then we'd have a perfect world."

"And God would be here already," Brian said, "but we can try to be just like love, can't we? I think the verses are an acid test for relationships; if we are not easily angered and keep no record of wrongs, can you imagine the kind of families we'd have?"

Maribel shrugged and placed the food on the counter. "I would have grown up differently, that's for sure. Would you like to eat now or later?"

Brian sat on the settee and remarked, "Later. You have a very nice apartment."

"Thanks," Maribel said feelingly. "Today my boss tried to take it away from me by encouraging me to quit."

"He did?" Brian said, aghast. "So why were you in such a buoyant mood when I called then?"

"I called his bluff, made him realize he was being an idiot."

Brian nodded and sat back relaxed. "That's terrific. So let me see you sing it."

"You mean do the impersonation and everything?" Maribel flushed. "I don't think I could go that far with a pastor in the house."

"It's not a pastor in the house; it's Brian in the house. Let's see you, Maribel."

Maribel shrugged. "Okay, if I let go and shock you, don't excommunicate me, okay?"

Brian laughed.

She pressed the pause button on the CD player and started dancing wildly to the first verse. When the second verse started she joined in.

She flung her head back and in true Tina Turner style belted out the last verse of the song, 'Ooh, how I love you, baby. '

Brian was looking at her, his eyes half closed; he was nodding his head and snapping his fingers. "Do you?" he asked huskily.

Maribel, breathing hard, flopped down in the settee opposite his. She closed her eyes; of course, she was growing to love him. Any fool could see that; did he love her was the question. And would he love her after he found out about her past was another question.

She looked at him. "My favorite text is, 'Beloved, let us love one another ... God orders me to love you, so I do.'"

Brian laughed softly. "Well ... I love you too."

They stared at each other for an eternity, unspoken feelings flowing in the air between them.

Brian cleared his throat. "I was thinking we could go out for ice cream after dinner."

Maribel nodded mutely. Her thoughts were treading along more lustful lines. She tried to rein them in, but gave up in the middle of her inward war and stood up abruptly. "I am going to have a long, cold shower."

Brian looked at her sharply. "Coming here was a bad idea, wasn't it? I feel like I need one too."

They ended up at Devon House, a 127-year-old heritage site in the middle of the city that was built by Jamaica's first black millionaire. After Maribel finished extolling the virtues of the ice cream there, and the unique shops on site, Brian dragged her into each of them, exclaiming softly at the merchandise found there. He was especially taken with the chocolate shop.

"Your tourist streak is showing," Maribel teased.

"This is a great place," Brian said as they headed toward the ice cream shop. "I love it here."

"When you taste the ice cream I'm sure that I will probably have to walk home."

"It's that good, huh?" Brian teased. "That I would leave the lovely Maribel, in bright pink blouse, to match her pink lips, to fend for herself in the city streets."

Maribel giggled.

"Well, what would you suggest?" They were in the quaint shop. It had a heady smell of pastry and the subdued scent of chocolate mixed with cherry. Brian was looking at the menu choices in awe. "Are you serious? They actually have sour sop ice cream."

"Yes, but I don't have anything else but rum and raisin," Maribel said seriously. "Lecture me later about the rum thing."

Brian grinned. "I will mark down this moment. You aren't a closet drunk, are you? An errant church sister that drinks a pint before bed?"

Maribel grinned. "No, I am not one of those, but this ..." she licked her lips when the attendant handed her a double scoop on a cone, "I could eat this every night, all night."

Brian ordered sour sop and coconut.

"I am sure that combination is weird," Maribel said, moaning low in her throat as she slowly licked the cream from the cone.

Brian looked at her, aghast. "Should I be watching this? Do you two want a room?"

Maribel looked at him wearily through half-closed lids. "Don't disturb me," she growled as they sat down on a bench.

Brian occasionally glanced at her as she slowly and methodically groaned and licked her way through the ice cream. His flavors were surprisingly good but he barely tasted them. Maribel was turning him on like he had never been turned on before. He had never been this attracted to a woman before. Throughout his life he tried to not base his relationship decisions on attraction alone; he firmly believed in the verse in the Bible that said, 'They that wait upon the Lord shall soar upon wings like eagles.'

He was going to have to pray seriously about her as his wife because as it was now he was very close to becoming the main headline for a gossip rag: 'Pastor Fondles Church Sister in Middle of Park'.

"I am writing a book." He pushed his mind from the carnal and focused on the spiritual.

Maribel wiped her mouth and smiled. "That was heavenly.

Do you think that there'll be ice cream in heaven?"

Brian shrugged. "I don't know, but certainly there'll be milk and honey."

"I always wondered if that would mean that there'll be cows and bees—you know, cows walking around with full udders of milk spewing as they walk and bees buzzing around honey combs while gold-teethed angels smile with you, constantly reflecting the gold from the street."

Brian laughed so hard that he toppled over his ice cream onto the grass. "Now look what you made me do," he gasped.

Maribel grinned at him. "I know that milk and honey means prosperity and all, but I always try to picture it literally, from my mortal and earthly point of view."

Brian wiped a drop of ice cream from his shirt.

"So what's your book about?" Maribel asked, referring to his earlier statement.

"It's a book about forgiveness," Brian said, still smiling. "I did some interviews with some church people over the years, compiling their testimonies about what we would call extreme forgiveness. Like this church sister whose son was shot in the head by his schoolmate. He died at hospital. The guy who shot him was caught by the police, and while in prison he was severely beaten and almost left for dead. She was his only visitor through his ordeal, and when he was released she took him in."

Maribel gasped, "Wow, talk about forgiveness."

Brian whistled, "I have some other hair-turning stories that will make you sit back and think about what God really asks us to do when he says forgive others their trespasses. If we don't forgive our fellow men he doesn't hear our prayers, you know."

"That's heavy duty stuff," Maribel said contemplatively, appraising him.

"After I tell the stories, I tie them in with Bible texts and stories."

"That sounds great," Maribel said brightly. She could challenge him with her past and see how well he dealt with forgiveness, but she was reluctant to spoil the mood of the evening. "When I joined the church I wrestled with the concept of forgiveness so I used to go to bed constantly with the passage from Hebrews 4:16 which says, 'Let us therefore come *boldly* unto the *throne of grace' I* finally realized that God didn't want me to doubt his forgiving power but to claim it knowing that he has forgiven me despite my past. I really needed that."

Brian nodded. "When did you join the church?"

"It was on my birthday three years ago. Cathy told me that I was going to the biggest party around. She was my roommate then."

"So you were a party girl, Maribel Contrell?"

Maribel laughed. "And how! I was the life of the party."

Brian grimaced. "Had many boyfriends, did you?"

Maribel looked at him seriously. "Would it be a problem if I said yes?"

Brian nodded. "Honestly, I can't say that I am not seething with jealousy."

Maribel smiled. "Actually, I never had many serious relationships." Most of them were fleeting and paying customers. Not that she would say the last part aloud.

She watched the relief creep across his face at her pronouncement and knew that she couldn't burst his bubble tonight. She'd probably need to tell him one day, though, before they got even closer.

Chapter Eleven

Women's Ministries meeting was packed when Maribel stepped into the church hall. She had missed the last couple of meetings and Cathy was walking beside her with a smirk on her face.

"So you went to Bible study with Pastor Brian last week Sunday, huh?"

"Yup," Maribel said, glancing around the room.

"Lovely to see you again, Sister Maribel," Sister Bertram gave her a hug, interrupting Cathy's probing.

"So are things serious?" Cathy asked as they sat in empty chairs arranged in a circle. "You have hardly called me all week and you only have time to say a breathy hello after church before you are whisked away by Pastor Handsome."

Maribel snickered. "I like him."

"You like him." Cathy frowned. "Like him? I don't believe it. Like is a very mild word to use to describe your behavior, young lady. I want you to spill all the beans."

"Well, after work couple weeks ago, I went with him for ice cream," Maribel whispered as she spotted Sister Thelma and her daughter Rose heading for them. "Here comes Sister Thelma."

"What are you two doing over here in a huddle?" Sister Thelma asked superiorly. "You aren't by any chance discussing the weather, are you?"

"When you came in I had the thought that it was about to get frosty with a hint of ice ... I mean snow," Cathy said cheekily as Thelma frowned.

"Well," Thelma fixed her blue hat on her head, "I don't find that funny, Cathy. There is no snow in Jamaica and if that is a swipe at me, I refuse to be offended this morning. You see Rose and I are going to a very important wedding."

Rose nodded. "Yes we are, a cousin of ours."

She sounded so pleasant to Maribel that she had to glance up quickly. Absent from her voice was the waspishness she had begun to expect from Sister Thelma. She seemed genuinely nice, and for a moment Maribel looked at her properly. She was really pretty, petite with a smooth caramel complexion. Her hair was cut in a pageboy style. It looked healthy and black and glistened in the light of the church hall.

"May we sit here?" she asked, gesturing at the chairs beside Maribel and Cathy.

"Sure," Cathy said, giving her a genuine smile. Maribel nodded and continued to look at her.

"It's not just any wedding," Thelma piped up loudly so that everyone in her vicinity could hear, "it is my brother's girl, Keisha, and as you all know my brother is a Senator in the House of Parliament and his wife Mildred is a Queens Counsel lawyer."

Cathy snorted loudly.

Thelma looked at her sharply. "Did I mention that the Prime Minister and several leaders of business will be there?"

"Mom," Rose said sternly, "I warned you about boasting; it is not right." She threw her hand up in the air. "I am going to sit beside Maribel."

She sat down beside Maribel and laughed softly. Her mother's face was set in stubborn lines. "No need to put space between us, Rose, I am not going to reveal anything else about our lives, but don't you think it is good to let your fellow sisters in Christ know what's going on in your life?"

Rose looked up in the air and then turned and looked at Maribel. "She is my thorn in the side, you know?"

Maribel smiled.

"I am pretty sure that all my accomplishments have been paraded for all to hear."

Maribel nodded. "Very much so."

"I barely made it through the Masters," Rose said, sighing. "I was tired, overworked and had a bad case of homesickness for all the time I was away. I resented more than anything that my mother had encouraged me to leave here to do it. I wanted to do it part-time, but she threw a fit."

All the time she was talking Maribel was thinking to herself, *She really is the opposite of her name-dropping mother, a genuinely nice person.*

"I was saying to Brian when he had dinner with us last week Tuesday that my mother needs prayers more than me or Gunther."

"You … you had dinner with Brian, er, Pastor Edwards last week?" Maribel almost choked on her words. She felt a shaft of jealousy shimmy through her that was so strong she almost fainted.

Was he courting Rose on the side? Was he flirting with her? Was he wondering which one of them would make the better pastor's wife? She suddenly felt hot and flushed. Rose would win hands down; she definitely didn't have a past like hers.

"Oh yes," Rose said, oblivious to Maribel's distress. "He is such a great guy, and handsome too. My mother is trying to fix us up. She is so blatant about it that I am scared she'll have him running in the other direction."

Cathy glanced at Maribel's face; she had been eavesdropping on the conversation while vaguely listening to Thelma's recount of all the influential people in her family. Maribel looked pale and shaky.

"I am going to a graduation with him this Sunday but only because my mother threw such pointed hints at him that he grudgingly offered the suggestion. I wish it was a date, though. Good men are so hard to find."

"Okay ladies," Sister Bertram clapped her hands, "let's begin. One would think that you hadn't seen each other for a whole week instead of just yesterday."

Maribel subsided in her chair and stared vacuously into space as Sister Bertram spoke.

"Are you all right?" Cathy whispered to her.

"No," Maribel said, sounding strangled.

Cathy patted her hand and turned as Sister Bertrand gushed, "There are a few of you who have certain talents in the cooking department, like Sister Carlene."

Carlene grinned and got up. "I made sugar-free, fat-free molasses cookies for Pastor Brian and took them on vestry day last week. He told me it was a vast improvement on cardboard. I promised him some more this week."

Snickers were coming from various parts of the room.

"I don't think that's a compliment," Thelma said loudly.

Carlene sat down huffily. "He doesn't like baked products. Can someone tell me if that is normal or natural? So I had to rethink my woo-him-with-baked-goods strategy."

"So he hasn't proposed yet, then?" Sister Greenwood asked seriously. Her hands gave her away because they were folded tightly in her lap, as if she was finding it really hard not to laugh.

"It's just one month," Carlene said optimistically.

"Watch out for Maribel and Rose," Sister Greenwood said, looking at both women. "I heard that he went out with Maribel on Monday and Rose on Tuesday."

Rose looked at Maribel and Maribel swallowed convulsively.

"You dark horse, you," Rose said, laughing. "Here I was telling you stuff, not knowing that you were seeing him."

Maribel grimaced. "I had no idea that the pastor had so many fans."

"You thought you were the only fan?" Rose asked incredulously. "Do you know how many of these wonderful sisters are after him, married and unmarried?"

Maribel whispered, "I had some indication at the first meeting but I had no idea that they were pursuing him so aggressively."

Rose whispered back, "A single pastor in a church full of women means war, Maribel. Until he chooses 'the one', he is fair game."

"I feel duly warned," Maribel said. "I might just throw up my hands and bow out of this so-called war. I doubt I'll ever be the one." Tears welled up in her eyes and she got up. "I need to go to the bathroom."

Rose nodded and watched her as she left the church hall in a rush.

Cathy got up too and followed.

Thelma had a pleased smile on her face as she moved to sit beside Rose. "I wonder if she's coming back."

"Of course," Rose said pleasantly, "she's a strong girl, would make a great friend. I wonder why on earth you told me those awful things about her."

Maribel was in the bathroom stall sobbing. She had no hope now; if she revealed her past to Brian he would just skip her over in selecting a wife. When had she started thinking that it would be okay to tell him?

Was she naïve or plain stupid? A hysterical laugh escaped her throat. She was never going to escape what had already happened in her life, and it was going to affect her future relationships—or lack thereof.

She dried her eyes and tried to toughen her resolve. She was a big girl; she had been on her own for years; she could handle this.

Cathy was standing at the sink when she came out. "Finished bawling now?"

Maribel nodded.

"You are a beautiful, intelligent woman. I don't see why you are so lacking in confidence that you would allow a few church sisters to move you to tears."

"You don't understand," Maribel mumbled, washing her face. "I have a past, I am no competition for the virgin Carlene, and have you seen Rose? She's really good-looking and intelligent and comes from a nice family and has connections, and did I say she was nice and has a pristine past? Spotless and unblemished … pure as the driven snow."

Cathy looked thoughtful. "But she has one fatal flaw."

"What?" Maribel asked, drying her face and looking at her red eyes in the mirror. She wasn't a pretty crier.

"She has a very annoying mother," Cathy said feelingly. "No amount of connections and niceness can make up for that. A man just has to picture Thelma permanently in his life and Rose is history."

Maribel sniffed. "What about Carlene?"

"Carlene?" Cathy frowned. "Are you crazy? Looks aside, even pastors consider their sex lives; it's an important part of marriage. Can you imagine Sister Carlene lying down stiffly, her hands at her side, singing *Beulah Land* during the sex act?"

Maribel started giggling and couldn't stop. "You are awful. How am I ever going to look at Carlene again with a serious expression?"

Cathy patted her back. "I think you are assuming too much where Brian is concerned. He seems to like you very, very much. What do you think all those gifts and things were for?"

"I got one on Tuesday," Maribel said, frowning. "The thirteenth gift was a picture of the two of us when we went to Independence Park. We had paid one of those camera men to take the picture."

Cathy nodded. "There you go. I have known Greg for two years and we are going to get married in four months and I have never received such a romantic gesture."

"But the point is that he went to dinner with Rose the same Tuesday," Maribel said, pouting.

"He went to dinner with Rose and her family," Cathy corrected. "Now come on, stop this past business and move on."

They walked back up to the church hall, smiling. After the meeting Thelma drew Maribel to one side and said solemnly, "Sister Maribel, I am so ashamed of myself. I talked to Rose about it and she said I should not tell you anything, but the Lord knows I have to get it off my chest."

"What is it?" Maribel asked wearily. Most people were standing around talking and were not paying them any undue attention.

"Well … I …" Thelma was wringing her hands and looking uncertain. "The truth is … I should just come out and say it, I guess. Well, you see, I was tidying up my son's room—God knows he's a slob."

Maribel frowned; why was she telling her this?

"Usually the helper would do it but it is so hard to find good help these days and my last helper just walked out of the house without a word. Anyway, I had to clean Gunther's room. It was a sty as usual but under his bed I took out several vdv boxes."

"Huh?" Maribel asked curiously. "What's vdv?"

"You know, those things that you put in the player and get good quality movies."

"Oh, you mean DVD?" Maribel asked, puzzled, wondering impatiently why Thelma had singled her out to tell her about Gunther.

"Yes, that's it." Sister Thelma's eyes lit up and she smoothed down her blue dress nervously. "Well, I was looking at the covers and cringing at the titles—you know, those pictures with naked girls in different poses."

Maribel nodded, a prickle of awareness crawling up her skin. Her head felt like it was on the verge of swelling and her palms began to sweat.

"I tell you," Thelma said dramatically, "on this box was a naked picture of a girl in thigh high black boots and nothing else, and as God is my witness, Sister Maribel, the title of the movie was *Peaches Quenches The Fire*." She shuddered. "The girl had on a blond wig and had about six men standing behind her in seductive naked poses. Holding their … " she leaned even closer to Maribel " … hoses. Can you imagine that?"

Maribel felt the breath sucking out of her body. "No," she

whispered hoarsely.

"Well, this girl … this Peaches looked just like you," Sister Thelma said, a note of horror creeping into her voice. "I could have sworn it was you. I tell you, Rose said that everybody has a double in this world, but what a thing, to have a double who is a porn star. It is such a shame and disgrace, an upstanding church sister like you having a porn star as a double. I had to shout Lord have mercy when I saw the shameful abomination."

Sister Thelma shook her head, "I am so happy that my Rose doesn't resemble a porn star. I am going to tell Gunther to take his trash out of my house once and for all."

Maribel cleared her throat. Her heart was beating a mile a minute and she felt nauseous. Her past had finally caught up with her.

"You must not allow that rubbish in your house," she said shakily to Thelma.

"I know dear," Thelma said, looking at her closely. "Are you well?"

"Not really," Maribel said. "I am just going to head home now and have a nap."

Chapter Twelve

Brian swung in his chair and contemplated the news he just heard from his mother. His father's chest pains had developed into a mild heart attack and his mother had been inconsolable. His sisters had tried to calm her down but he had just hung up the phone on a very distraught lady. He felt like going back home now. His mother literally fell apart without male support and with his father ill he did not want her to have a nervous breakdown and give his father another heart attack.

There was so much news for him to process now; Pastor Green, the pastor who was now in his circuit of churches in Canada, had developed a terrible case of pneumonia and was making noises that he wanted to come back home.

"It is as cold as a witch's tit up here, Brian," he had said irreverently, his breathing over the phone sounding like an old truck that needed tuning.

"I am just fifty," he had wheezed down the phone, "and I

feel like ninety now. The cold over here is going to kill me."
He had coughed after that, a big wracking, gurgling sound
that had Brian thinking he really was dying.

"It's not too late to switch back," Pastor Green had hacked
out, his voice petering out as he struggled for breath. "I
already spoke to the conference heads and they agree."

No doubt, Brian had thought, *after they heard you speaking.*

He had hung up from that conversation and his thoughts
had immediately switched to Maribel. He had been praying
about a relationship with her and had asked the Lord to
give him a sign, but for the past two weeks she had been
avoiding him. He was wondering if that was his sign. He was
immensely attracted her—her love for God, her smile, her
walk, her sense of humor and how when he thought about
her he ran out of superlatives.

Her birthday was next Sunday, which unfortunately for
him coincided with his cousin's wedding, a wedding that he
was participating in as the best man. And it was in Negril, a
place that he knew Maribel associated with some amount of
trauma from her past.

He didn't want to leave her behind either, but the invitation
did say Brian Edwards and guest. He wanted her to be his
guest. Whenever they went out together he had more fun
and felt a lightness that was quite unique. He had this
unshakeable feeling that she was 'the one' and when a man
found 'the one' he did not wait around for long.

He considered all his alternatives. His father was ill and his
mother was frantic; Pastor Green was ill and wanted to come
back home. It seemed to him that all roads led to Canada. He
had to run it by Maribel and see if she wanted to move to
Canada. He would propose on her birthday. Have a simple
wedding in church here and then a reception at his church in
Canada; tie up all loose ends and then leave. He needed to

pin her down. She claimed that she was tired in the nights when she came home and missed two weeks from church because of various ailments. He would have to surprise her and take her to lunch.

Maribel stared at the numbers floating across her computer screen. One of the partners, Mr. Hayles, had stopped at her office and complimented her on her work on the Hodges Construction account but it did not put a dent in the prevailing depression that shrouded her like a cloak, a tight suffocating cloak.

After Thelma had slyly tried to find out if she was a porn queen, she had this feeling of impending doom—that any minute now her world was going to explode into tiny fragments around her.

She had tried to avoid Brian but he emailed, texted and called her incessantly. Damn the information age. She couldn't escape him and she couldn't escape her dratted naked photos. Every time she thought that she had some peace, her past kept popping up somewhere.

She opened her computer browser and typed in "Peaches Jamaica" and up popped her image on five DVD covers, the very first images on Google's search engine. She squeezed her eyes shut. The pictures were clearly of her—stark naked. She hurriedly closed the page and wiped it from the computer's history.

If it was on the Internet, it was there forever; hundreds of men and women had probably looked at it from around the world. She had never thought to search for her images before and now that she had, she felt like a prisoner condemned to hang.

Her past deeds would forever be a rope around her neck,

wouldn't they? She continually ran through the thoughts in her head until she felt a pain gathering in the region of her chest. She liked to think that her heart couldn't take it anymore and was about to give way; they would find her dead in the office. Dead of a heart attack just a week before her twenty-fifth birthday.

Some smart person would start searching for her next of kin and would sniff around Negril until they came upon the truth that Maribel and Peaches were the same person. But it wouldn't matter then because she'd be dead. All her friends and acquaintances could judge her then. She wouldn't care. She wouldn't give a …

"Maribel," Vivian stuck her head around the door, "I got chocolates from England so here's yours."

"Paul's mother is here, then?" Maribel asked, trying to inject some enthusiasm in her voice.

"Came last night," Vivian said, placing the box of chocolates on the desk. "Apparently Paul told her that I am a chocolate lover. She carried her hand luggage full of it."

"Okay," Maribel said, turning back to her computer.

"You are going to tell me what is wrong with you," Vivian demanded sternly. "I am getting tired of you walking around with a hangdog expression on your face. I know it's not Mark that's bothering you because I heard through the grapevine that he was caught en flagrante with this chick in Marketing. It's being hushed up though, so he is very scarce around here."

Maribel smiled. "His wife needs to know about him."

Vivian shrugged. "Enough about that; tell me about you."

"I will," Maribel said, sighing, "just not today and not in this office."

"Okay," Vivian said appeased, "I will let you off the hook for now, but until you recover that great smile of yours, I am going to keep on asking."

Maribel gave her a wan look. "Thanks for caring, Viv."

"That's what friends do." Vivian went through the door and gave her a thumbs-up sign.

Her phone rang at the same time and she picked it up. "Hello."

"I won't take no for an answer; can we do lunch today?" Brian greeted her. "And before you find some excuse to deny me the pleasure of your company, I will carry the lunch and camp out in your parking lot."

Maribel felt the first bloom of happiness gather in her chest and tried to squelch it. But it wasn't responding to her, it just kept blossoming like a flower unfolding its petals and suddenly all was right with her day.

"No camping out in parking lots for you today. Where are we going for lunch?"

"I'll pick you up," Brian said mysteriously. "At 12:30," he added belatedly.

"Looking forward to it," Maribel whispered.

They were seated in the air-conditioned comfort of a tropical themed restaurant, complete with parrots and water fountains. They had just ordered drinks and Maribel was looking around and playing with her straw. The middle of the straw was in the shape of a pineapple and she found it fascinating to watch the yellow liquid fill up the pineapple pouch before it reached her lips.

Brian was watching her intently before he cleared his throat. "How long do we have?" He looked at his watch and frowned. "Is it just me or is the day flying by at supersonic speed?"

"It's just you," Maribel said, laughing at him. "My day is

dragging by so slowly that I am beginning to think of work as punishment. That's why I took the rest of the day off."

"You did?" Brian's face lit up. "Are you going to spend it with me?"

Maribel shrugged and then laughed at his crestfallen expression. "I am all yours."

Brian cleared his throat. "You know, I have been praying about that, Maribel."

"Praying about what?" Maribel asked, feeling nervous about the urgency in his voice.

"About you being mine. And I think I have gotten my answer."

"What's the answer?" Maribel asked with bated breath, her heart pounding.

"Your answer I want to be yes; my question is, will you marry me?"

Maribel gasped.

Brian was tense as he watched the play of expressions over her face.

"Do … do … I have to answer now?" Maribel asked, a cowardly feeling overtaking her. "I have to tell you something about me first."

"So tell," Brian said, smiling at her and taking her hand in his.

"I can't tell you now," Maribel said, grimacing.

"Can you tell me on our way to Negril this Sunday coming? I have a wedding to go to and I would like you to be my guest."

Maribel withdrew her hand from his and didn't get the chance to answer, as a waiter came to take their order.

"Tofu in jerk sauce," Brian said, smiling, "with lots of raw vegetables and rice and peas."

"Same for me," Maribel said to the waiter. She was in

shock and wasn't thinking straight. *A pastor asked me to marry him. A pastor asked me to marry him. Brian asked Maribel to marry him. Oh my God!* She even ordered tofu and she didn't like it. She was in real trouble.

"So will you go to Negril with me?" Brian asked Maribel, a tinge of anxiety in his tone.

Maribel sighed. "Why not?"

Brian exhaled. "So what do you want us to do for the rest of the day? I can clear my appointments until five o'clock."

Maribel whistled. "I want to play mini golf and eat ice cream and forget …"

Brian looked at her. "I hope you are not trying to forget my proposal?"

Maribel laughed. "Never that, I assure you—never that."

Chapter Thirteen

Thelma did not like loose ends and the issue of Maribel so closely resembling a porn queen was a loose end she was not going to leave alone. She stood in her living room, pondering the situation. From the moment she had seen that girl Maribel, she had known that something was not right.

Could it be that Maribel Contrell from Westmoreland was indeed a prostitute? She felt all the hairs on her neck standing up in delicious anticipation of the possibilities. She had not rested well since she saw that picture and indeed had hidden the box in the back of her closet.

The more she secretly took it out and looked at it, the more she was sure that the image was of Maribel. It was two weeks since her find, and day and night she checked to make sure that the box was safely in her closet. Her husband Horace had found her actions amusing and laughed at her scornfully when she mentioned her suspicions but she knew, deep down, that there was no way that somebody could resemble another person so closely without there being a strong connection. The girl on the cover even had Maribel's slanted eyes. Even though on the cover the eyes were emphasized with heavy kohl, she could see that they were the same eyes. The eyes don't lie.

She rubbed her hands together in glee. Today she was going to do something about her suspicions. She was going to investigate and despite what Horace and Rose said, she was going to get to the bottom of the mystery.

She paced her spacious living room in a frenzy, trying to formulate a plan to go through with the investigation. "Where is the first place to do some sleuthing?" she asked her cat, who was cleaning itself on the carpet.

The cat ignored her and Thelma snapped her fingers. "Why don't I call the company that made the pictures?"

"I am so smart," she said to her husband, who was coming through to the living room, a briefcase in hand and a frantic look on his face.

"Thelma," he growled, "leave the issue alone; if the girl was a prostitute she has obviously turned her life around and is trying to move on. Why are you still bemoaning the issue?"

Thelma sighed, "You don't get it; this is a girl the pastor likes and spends time with—when he does that he has no time for Rose. I knew from the moment she walked into Women's Ministries meeting that she was going to be trouble. I saw it imprinted on her face."

Horace sighed and sat down on a chair, opening his briefcase. "Let Rose choose her own man."

"Didn't you like him when he came to dinner?" Thelma demanded of Horace.

"Of course, he seems like a good man." Horace caressed his beard contemplatively. "Very modest and well spoken and obviously dedicated to his ministry."

"Exactly," Thelma snapped her fingers. "He is a cut above the rest and handsome too, a nice foil for my Rose."

Horace sighed and placed his glasses on his nose as he peered through some papers. "It just seems un-Christian-like that you are tearing down another person for your own gains."

"I am not tearing down another person," Thelma snorted. "I am just going to investigate exactly what it is that this woman has to hide. And if she is a porn queen she can't be a pastor's wife, that's for sure—so that's one opportunist out of the way."

Thelma headed upstairs and then looked back over her shoulders to her husband, who was busy sorting through business documents. "Do you see how the Lord can use the things that seem so bad to teach us a lesson?"

Horace grunted.

"Look at how Gunther watches his filth and I complain day in and day out. Out of that filth has arisen a beautiful mystery."

"It might not be her, you know," Horace said, looking up, "I pray to God it isn't because with you on her case she might not want to live when you are through."

Thelma laughed gaily. "I will take that as a compliment to my tenacity and cut- throat business acumen."

"I am out of here," Horace stood up. "I have a meeting with one Mr. Mark Ellington now. His accounting firm will be handling our business from now on."

Thelma waved cheerily. "Have a blessed day, honey."

Horace half smiled. "I wish you the same." He closed the front door and Thelma ran up the stairs and headed for the closet. She took the now-familiar box out of her closet and examined the back.

"Peaches, the Hot Jamaican Diva ... visits the firehouse to put out the firemen's fire."

Thelma blushed; she had never really read the back before. But there was another picture of Peaches sitting on a fire truck between two men. She hurriedly flicked through the text: produced and directed by Jamrotic Limited.

These days if you wanted to find anything you had to go to the Internet. She booted up her laptop. *Of course Jamrotic would have a number listed online; they had a website listed.*

She fidgeted nervously until the computer booted up and she could get to an Internet browser. Her instinct was telling her, stronger than ever, that despite the blonde wig and exaggerated makeup, this was Maribel.

She typed in Jamrotic and it loaded quickly. She grimaced when she saw the pictures and videos that were loaded on her screen. "Why do people love this filth?" she moaned. She clicked on 'about us' and found two numbers, one in Jamaica and one in America. She quickly scribbled down the numbers and closed the page; just being on the page made her feel somewhat dirty.

Thelma hurriedly dialed the Jamaican number and a male voice answered.

"Hello." She cleared her throat. "I just saw a video with a girl named Peaches and I was wondering if I could book her for some modeling assignments."

"We don't work with Peaches no more," said the heavily-accented American voice.

"Oh," Thelma said hurriedly, praying that the man did not hang up. "Do you know where I can contact her or what her real name is?"

The man fumbled on the phone and then she heard swearing in the background. "She stole our money and ran away, man, she and her friend Cream—or was it Cream that stole the money and ran away with Peaches? I can't remember; they're all bitches."

Thelma winced. "Oh, could you tell me her real name?"

"I think it was Fiona or Felicia or some ish like that."

Thelma clutched the phone tighter. "Fiona or Felicia?" she asked incredulously.

"Yeah," the man over the phone said drowsily, "bitch took my money and ran away. I heard she is dead though, but that's a'ight."

"Oh okay," Thelma said, disappointed. "Thank you."

She hung up the phone feeling ridiculously let down; she could have sworn that it was Maribel that was on the DVD cover. She sat down and processed what the guy said. There was a girl who called herself Peaches and one called Cream. Peaches' real name was Fiona or Felicia, not Maribel.

What a disappointment—or was it? Thelma thought craftily. She could get Maribel to come to dinner tomorrow and then find out about her past. After all, she could have given the wrong name to the men when she went filming.

She was not giving up until she exposed little Miss Maribel once and for all.

Maribel hurriedly gathered her papers together and threw them in her file folder. Mark had just popped his head around the door and told her that she had to attend a meeting with a new client.

"He's one Mr. Lawrence, the major partner in the law firm Lawrence and Rich. If we bag this one, I am going to assign Vivian the Hodges account and you this account, so you have to be there."

So Maribel was now heading for her meeting, her grey suit wrinkle-free and every single strand of hair in place. She had to be circumspect when it came to meeting new clients and this for her was a rare treat. Mark was the one who handled new clients but since he intended for her to manage the account he wanted her to sit in. *He must have grown some brains since I threatened him,* Maribel thought smugly as she headed for his office. Either that, or he was expecting her to screw up, so that he could legitimately fire her.

She stepped into the conference room and sat down opposite Mark around the table, which could comfortably seat thirty persons. This was where prospective clients were taken for their first meeting.

Mark looked at her balefully. "I guess I don't need to tell you that you are now representing the firm so you have to be on your best behavior."

Maribel barely resisted the urge to roll her eyes. The words arrogant and pig-headed kept floating in her head and she felt like leaning over the table and strangling him.

What did he expect her to do, start trashing the building like a maniac or hike up her skirt to flash the representatives? She knew that she gave her all to her work and did a good job; why did this chauvinistic pig think otherwise?

She bared her teeth in the semblance of a smile and murmured, "You will not have to worry about me."

He inclined his head and his eyes ran over her face. "You are looking especially good today."

Maribel was saved from a reply when Mark's secretary showed three men through the door.

Mark stood up and pouring on the phony business charm, which he reserved for his business meetings; he introduced himself and Maribel.

"And this is the main partner in Lawrence and Rich, Horace Lawrence."

Maribel smiled at Horace Lawrence politely. "Nice to meet

you Mr. Lawrence."

Horace smiled when he saw her. "I am actually a frequent visitor of your church, my dear. I believe you know my wife Thelma and my daughter Rose."

Maribel smiled, "Yes, I do know them."

Horace laughed heartily. "Mark here spoke so highly of your talents that we had to invite you to this meeting."

"Thank you," Maribel replied politely, inwardly seething. Mark the snake had acted as if her sitting on in the meeting was his idea.

"So, let's get down to business, shall we?" Horace said genially. He looked at Maribel a little longer than was polite and thought to himself it was no wonder Thelma was obsessed with the girl; she was beautiful and had that air of vulnerability that men found so attractive. He sincerely hoped that she was not the porn star that his wife was so certain she was, because that would make business between the firms untenable.

He was no judge and he tended to leave all judging to God when it came to people's lives but if it was proven that Maribel was the girl in those pictures, Thelma, who was a major shareholder in the business, would not let him rest if Maribel was the accountant handling the firm's money.

Chapter Fourteen

"**O**h Sister Maribel," Thelma had called her in the evening just after she had stepped into her apartment, "I am inviting you to dinner this evening. My husband told me the wonderful news that you will be handling our company's accounts."

"Oh yes," Maribel said, feeling the apprehension that settled on her shoulders starting to weighing her down.

"I am leaning toward a seven o'clock dinner."

Maribel wanted to tell Thelma to go to hell but that wouldn't be polite, and now she had the added burden of a business interest, she would have to be on her best behavior. Thelma's revelation that she had seen someone on a DVD cover who looked like her still haunted her at night. She had nightmares where everyone would find out her past and mock her or worse, treat her like a pariah.

"I invited Pastor Brian too," Thelma giggled girlishly, "and of course Rose will be here."

Maribel sighed; she had wanted to go walking with Brian

this evening. She loved it when they walked together and shared sallies and stories. Now she was stuck with Thelma Lawrence for one whole evening—the equivalent of hell.

"Well, seven o'clock it is, then," said Maribel forcing a little cheerfulness into her voice.

When Thelma hung up the phone Maribel couldn't help but feel as if she was planning something. From the first day she met Thelma she had shown open dislike toward her and now she was inviting her to dinner. How weird was that? And inviting Brian too? Even scarier was the thought.

What was she planning to do, show one of the DVDs with Maribel in it for entertainment and then have a quiz show afterward asking who does the porn star remind you of?

Maribel felt a shiver pass through her body. She searched through her closet and found a nice long dress. It was so long you could barely see her toes. It fitted her shape loosely and looked elegant enough. At least Thelma couldn't condemn her for dressing suggestively.

The phone rang and Maribel picked it up reluctantly. The news she seemed to be getting these days were not necessarily good.

"Hey," Brian said, his honey voice trickling smoothly through the phone line, "I heard that Sister Thelma got to you too."

"Oh yes," Maribel snorted, "and I just know I am going to regret this dinner some way or another."

Brian groaned, "Why is it that she rubs everyone the wrong way? Should I pick you up?"

"Sure," Maribel glanced at the clock. "I am going to have to hurry to get ready; it's now six o'clock."

"Okay, see you at quarter to seven. She lives in the hills. It should take us about fifteen minutes to get there, provided there is no traffic."

"All right then," Maribel hung up the phone, smiling.

She hummed in the shower as she thought about being Mrs. Brian Edwards. She would wear a white dress to her wedding, they would have a lovely honeymoon where she could act the shy virgin, and then they would have babies together.

No one had to know that she was a former prostitute and as the years wore on and they celebrated their fiftieth anniversary or when either of them was on a deathbed she would confess—people create their happily-ever-afters all the time, and she would have hers too. One day, she would probably even migrate and leave her Jamaican memories behind. She could start over afresh and she wouldn't have to confess her past.

But could she live like that? Of course, thousands of women did it every day; they kept secrets that their spouses would not believe. She could do it too. She loved Brian and she didn't see why she should spend her life a victim of her past. Let it stay buried and she would move on. With those thoughts in mind she happily applied lip gloss and brushed out her hair.

Horace and Thelma Lawrence lived in a mansion in Beverley Hills. They had a vast lawn area with nicely manicured shrubs and trees and an elegantly designed house with lots of glass windows overlooking the city.

Brian was telling her about the book he was writing and how interesting the concept of forgiveness was for Christians and people in general. She had sat and stared at him as he spoke, his eyes alight with excitement. He obviously was into his pet subject and she sat and listened and interjected with points that made him smile; before she knew it they were at Thelma's mansion. The gleaming black Mercedes that she had asked them to pray about in Women's Ministries was parked in the driveway.

"Welcome to my humble abode," Thelma said grandly when they went to the stylish front door. "Come on in, make yourselves at home."

Maribel reluctantly walked through to the living room behind Thelma, who was in a flowing yellow dress. She clutched Brian's hand when they sat down on the elegant sofas but was forced to release him after Thelma looked at their linked fingers with a sneer, her plucked eyebrows rising critically.

"Horace darling," she got up as her husband entered the room, "this is Maribel, as you know." She paused when she glanced at Maribel. "And our beloved pastor."

Rose entered the fray soon after that, coming down the stairs in a white off the shoulder blouse and a pin stripe work skirt.

After greetings and the banal polite chatter, which was causing every nerve ending in Maribel's body to draw tight as a guitar string in anticipation of the moment when Thelma would show up her true colors, she wasn't surprised when Thelma suddenly said, "My gosh, you know what I was thinking today when Horace told me you were the one handling our business accounts?"

"What?" Maribel asked politely. Her heart was beating a mile a minute as she watched Thelma's conniving eyes.

Thelma giggled, a high pitched sound that was grating on Maribel's last nerve. "I was thinking that we don't know enough about your past."

"Thelma," Horace said warningly.

"What dear?" Thelma asked, looking at her husband innocently. "Isn't it important that you should know if your accountant was an embezzler or not?"

"Fisher and Smith is a good company and Maribel comes highly recommended," Horace said, aggrieved.

"Are you trying to imply that she is an embezzler?" Brian asked, frowning.

"Excuse my mother a minute." Rose stood up and practically dragged Thelma from the room.

Horace looked embarrassed.

Brian looked at her, baffled.

Maribel stared into her glass and thought about all the things she wished she could do to Thelma. The woman was pure evil. She was hell-bent on exposing her and Maribel just realized what a foolish thing she had done by coming to this dinner. What if Thelma had already spread the news that she thought that Maribel was a porn star? Her career would be over.

"What's going on here?" Brian asked the room in general.

Horace leaned back in his chair. "I am not really sure. I thought we were here to have dinner."

He glanced at Maribel and then looked back at Brian. "Are you two together or something? I don't mean to be impolite but I think that your association with each other has created quite an interest on my wife's part, and as a busybody church sister she has taken it up on herself to vet Maribel's character."

Brian smiled, relieved; for a minute there he was thinking that Maribel had been involved in some embezzlement and that Thelma was trying to expose her. It didn't help that Maribel said she had something to tell him before she accepted his proposal. His mind was working overtime trying to figure out what it could be.

"Well, we are dating. I loved her from the moment I saw her," Brian said happily. "I really want to marry her."

"Ah," Horace nodded, "I could see the attraction when I saw you two together. So are you two going to get married?" Horace looked at Maribel.

Maribel smiled, "I will let him know first and then everyone else."

Horace nodded. "Fair enough."

"Dinner is ready." Thelma swooped into the room as if nothing had happened. "Come this way for me, please."

Everyone got up and trooped after her into a vast dining room with glass windows that overlooked the city lights. Thelma had turned down the lights so that the effect of the view could be enhanced. The dining room table was not a small one, as it seated about twelve persons comfortably. Horace sat at the head, Thelma to his right and Rose to his left. Maribel sat beside Thelma and across from Brian, a move that she was sure Thelma planned carefully.

Thelma's helper, Karen, was eager to please, as she was recently hired and was on probation. Thelma had whispered that information after the nervous-looking girl had served the appetizers and was heading for the kitchen.

She served some kind of soup with vegetables. It tasted bland to Maribel but she choked down a few spoonfuls because she was aware that Karen's job could very well be on the line if she appeared not to like it.

The next course was an improvement on the last. All the dishes were vegetarian—to impress Brian, she was sure.

Rose was having some kind of whispered conversation with Brian that Maribel could barely hear. Thelma glanced at her with a stony kind of warmth in her eyes. It was the look Maribel could imagine a snake having when it was trying to be nice.

"So Maribel," Thelma started her conversation as she carefully piled rice on her fork with her knife, "where in

Westmoreland are you from?"

Maribel twitched uncomfortably. "I lived in several places in Westmoreland." She swallowed.

Brian looked up from Rose's whispering and said heartily, "Maribel is from Negril. Coincidentally, that's where my grandparents are from too. And this Sunday Maribel and I are going to a wedding there."

"Ooooh," Thelma said excitedly, "that's a great place to relax with all those white sand beaches and gentle breezes. Perfect wedding spot." She looked over at her husband, a smile of victory on her face. "I think I am going to have to force Horace to take me there tomorrow."

Maribel felt as if her throat closed over. Why did Brian have to blurt it out like that? He knew how she felt about Negril. Now this evil witch knew exactly where she was from. *God help me*, a panicked voice kept ringing in her head.

Horace frowned. "I was thinking of going golfing with my friends over in St. Ann, Thelma."

"Tomorrow is a holiday, isn't it?" Rose asked bewilderedly. "I can barely tell the days apart since I got the promotion, they work me so hard at that place. I was just telling Brian that I am thinking of changing professions and working as a kindergarten teacher in the church school."

Horace coughed heavily and Thelma looked over at Rose, a contemplative gleam in her eye.

Maribel released a sigh of relief. Rose might be in contention for Brian's attention but she sure was working hard to take the heat off her. Every time her mother went into attack mode she threw her off Maribel's scent. She was so protective and kind. She reminded her a bit of Felicia.

"You know, Rose," Maribel said, trying to return the favor—Horace looked like he was about to blow on hearing about the career change and Thelma's left eye was ticking.

"You remind me so much of my friend Felicia. She was such a nice person."

Rose smiled at Maribel, recognizing the ploy for what it was.

Thelma stiffened in her chair, the fork she was unconsciously clutching fell from her fingers. All thoughts of Rose throwing away her hard earned MBA to teach snotty-nosed children fled from her thoughts and her mind ran over the conversation that she had with that uncouth lout on the phone from Jamrotic.

"I think it was Fiona or Felicia or some ish like that."

"Fiona or Felicia?" she asked incredulously.

"Yeah," the man over the phone said drowsily, "bitch took my money and ran away. I heard she dead though but that's a'ight."

What were the odds, Lord? She thought to herself, two girls; one called herself Peaches, the other Cream. She deserved a pat on her shoulder. Maribel was Peaches and Felicia was Cream. The only thing she needed now was concrete proof from the wonderful town of Negril.

"Dear," she said to Rose, a smile on her face, "I think that you should follow your heart's desire." She looked at Brian significantly. "Horace, you need to spend more time with your wife. I veto golf and say let's head to Negril."

Horace grumbled good-naturedly.

"So where is your friend now, Maribel?" Thelma asked with bated breath, willing the girl to say that she was dead.

"Oh, she died," Maribel said thickly, "on my birthday six years ago."

"That's so sad," Thelma said, a little bud of glee bubbling in her heart. It was her! It was really Maribel on that filthy DVD cover.

"I have peach and chocolate mousse with a hint of mint

cream for dessert," Thelma said to the table at large. "Anyone interested?"

"Sounds yummy," Rose said enthusiastically.

Brian smiled. "Sounds innovative."

Thelma laughed. "And you, Maribel, I hope you will enjoy it. It is the classic combination of peaches and cream."

She watched Maribel's frozen expression and had to suppress a very hearty laugh.

"Does anyone take their lunch break at 4:00?" Vivian asked two days later.

She glanced at Maribel, who was playing in her food; she was placing curried chicken on one side of the plate and rice on the other.

"Are you going to tell me what's wrong?" Vivian asked, concerned. "The other day I asked you and you went off to lunch with your boyfriend. When you returned you were on top of the world. Today you are back to being morose. You have hardly said a word to me."

"Is morose the word of the day?" Maribel asked, concentrating on getting all the chicken gravy away from her rice.

"No," Vivian growled, "the word of the day is something your Christian ears can't take if you don't tell me what's wrong."

Maribel looked up and then looked around the cafeteria. From her vantage point in the back she could see that the large room was empty. They had a good view of the heavy traffic meandering the New Kingston streets below. "In a nutshell, my life is ruined."

"How? Why?" Vivian asked urgently. "I thought we had gotten rid of Mark and his …"

"Not that," Maribel sighed and massaged her temples. "Brian asked me to marry him."

"I would jump up and say congratulations," Vivian said somberly, "but you just said that as if it is the end of the world."

"The story begins with me wanting to join more activities in the church, so I went to a Women's Ministries meeting."

"Which was a good and noble effort," Vivian said loyally.

Maribel smiled. "Then I met one Thelma Lawrence."

"Same surname as the Lawrence account ... She goes to your church?"

"Yup," Maribel nodded her head. "She hates me."

"I thought all church people were loving and kind."

Maribel laughed and slapped Vivian's hand. "I know you know that's a joke."

"Anyway, she has marked me as competition to her daughter, even before I even met the girl."

"The plot thickens." Vivian slurped her milkshake.

"The problem is…" Maribel wondered if she should tell Vivian about her past. And then she decided to just do it. If she didn't share this with her she was going to explode. And it didn't seem much like a secret anymore since Thelma was hinting at peaches and cream. She was just anxiously waiting for the ax to fall.

"The problem is … "

Vivian nodded eagerly.

"The problem is … I was a prostitute six years ago. I also did several porn videos. Nude pictures and you name it, I've done it."

Vivian stared at Maribel, wide eyed. "You? I thought you were a virgin."

Maribel laughed so hard that tears started seeping from her eyes. "What am I going to do, Viv? Thelma saw a DVD case with my picture on the front."

Vivian still sat there in shock. "When you say a prostitute, do you mean one of those girls that work on the street? I mean ... my God ... I mean ..."

"Yes," Maribel nodded. "I used to work on the street picking up strange men, giving them what they wanted for various prices."

"But you look so ... so ... normal. I am sorry ... " Vivian said, stammering. "I'm so sorry, I can't think. Just give me a few minutes to let it sink in."

Maribel nodded and watched as Vivian closed her eyes and leaned back in her chair. Vivian was not a Christian, didn't even go to church except on Easter and Christmas, and she was shocked. She didn't hold out much hope for anybody else. It would be over with her and Brian before she even managed to explain why her lifestyle had been the way it was. She wiped her eyes and looked over at the traffic.

Yesterday they had gone to a church social. He was concerned about his father's health but otherwise he was happy. His eyes lit up when he saw her, a look of such intense concentration that Maribel was sure she would never see that expression in any other man's eyes ever again. He made her feel as if she was the only woman in the room; he made her feel as if she was the only woman in the world.

"You have to tell Brian." Vivian opened her eyes and looked at Maribel intently.

Maribel nodded.

"He'll be hopping mad."

Maribel nodded again.

"Can you imagine? He's a pastor, for crying out loud. Some of them may not be living up to the expectations we have of them, but dang girl, this is deep. If you had just been a regular prostitute ... things would not be as bad ...

he wouldn't have to know ... but a prostitute starring in her own movies."

"Ex-prostitute," Maribel snorted.

Vivian laughed. "Ex-prostitute. And that is the point: you are an ex-prostitute and not currently one; that should be a point in your favor."

"I starred in a show called Fire quenchers or something like that," Maribel sighed. "Viv, this is not a joke; it was an orgy with six men. If I tell Brian ... we are through."

Vivian nodded. "True, but imagine not telling him. You have videos out there, Maribel, and you have a church sister who is sifting through your life. You have to beat her to telling him or you will look very bad in his eyes."

Maribel slumped her shoulders and pushed away her plate. "I could get fired for this."

"How?" Vivian asked.

"Picture this: Horace Lawrence whispers to Mark that I was a prostitute ... or a porn star."

Vivian sighed. "This sucks. I would recommend that you look for a job in another parish."

"Or country," Maribel said dejectedly. "Who will hire me? If I tell them that I used to work for Fisher and Smith they will call for a background check—Mark will surely spill the beans."

"Change jobs," Vivian said urgently.

"And do what?" Maribel asked. "I can't keep running away from my life and having people judge me based on my past."

"Atta girl," Vivian said enthusiastically, "that's the spirit. Fight back. Don't just leave things hanging and wait for the shoe to fall. Pre-empt the shoe. Beat Thelma at her game. Take the wind out of her sails."

"And lose Brian?" Maribel asked in a small voice.

"My advice to you, Sister Maribel," Vivian said cheekily,

"is to ask God what to do. Isn't that what Christianity is about, turning to God in times of peace but especially in times of trouble?"

"I feel as if he doesn't like me anymore," Maribel said, whining.

Vivian grabbed her hands earnestly. "It sounds to me as if you don't like you anymore. I still like you and I am just human. And as far as I understand it, isn't God bigger than your problems? The thought for the day on the notice board is 'Don't tell God how big your storm is, tell the storm how big your God is.'"

"I never read the notice board," Maribel said, getting up. "I had no idea they had those lovely thoughts on there." She hugged Vivian. "Thank you."

Chapter Fifteen

It was raining when they set out for Negril. Brian's total concentration had to be on the road. He listened to Maribel's chitchat with a sense of satisfaction. This was how it would be if they were married. She had looked so graceful in her jeans and top when she entered the car with a grin on her face.

"I had to carry two dresses." She had hung the garment bag on the rail above one of the back doors, revealing a slither of smooth belly skin. "I couldn't choose between pink and red."

He had laughed with her, very sure that his besotted look was pleading with her to tell him yes to his marriage proposal. He had been on tenterhooks all week long, wondering what she had to tell him and why it was so hard to say yes to him.

He had thought of several scenarios as to why she would delay saying yes, but none of them made sense.

She didn't have a boyfriend. As far as he could tell from

the church grapevine, which his secretary was very much a part of, she joined the church three years ago and rebuffed all the single brothers who were bold enough to approach her.

She was a perfect hostess; she had hosted a small get-together for him at his home last week and everyone enjoyed themselves; she could sing like an angel; she was so gracious and kind, animals and children loved her; she prayed with a conviction that indicated to him that God was her friend. She went with him to Bible studies and she was so circumspect and proper—they held hands but no kissing or inappropriate touching ever happened.

So what on earth could be wrong? She was, to him, perfect in every way. He was reluctant to approach the subject again. He didn't want to be rebuffed so he was patiently waiting for her to bring it up; she had promised him that today would be the day his questions would be answered.

When they reached Spur Tree Hill the visibility was so poor that Brian had to stop for a while. He pulled over on the side of the road and turned off the engine.

"What time is it?"

Maribel glanced at the dashboard. "Your clock says eight o'clock and my watch says 8:10."

"Just about two and a half hours to go," Brian yawned. "I love road trips, don't you?"

"No," Maribel grimaced. "I especially don't like road trips to Negril."

"Because it is the scene of the crime?" Brian adjusted his seat and leaned back, looking at her contemplatively.

Maribel turned in her seat and looked at him. He was freshly shaven and had that clean, fresh look that she liked to see on a man. He was so gorgeous and strong and good; why was she prolonging the agony of being with him? She should just tell him. Now would be the perfect time. They couldn't go any farther until the heavy fog dissipated somewhat and this was halfway to Kingston, so she could get a ride back if he kicked her out.

"It is the scene of the crime." Maribel sighed, "Brian, I have something to tell you."

Brian looked at her worried expression and froze. "Is it going to be no to my proposal?" He could feel his heart picking up speed. He could hear one thump after another, increasing in speed and frequency.

Maribel hesitated. "The truth is I am not as ... er ... my past is ... er ... this is hard."

"You are not saying no, are you?" Brian's eyes were sad. He kept thinking, *so this is what rejection feels like.*

"I am not saying no." Maribel fidgeted in her seat. "I am just saying that there are some really..."

Brian released the breath he was holding. "Thank God, for a minute there I thought you were going to turn me down flat. I haven't missed the fact that you haven't said yes either."

"You see ... " Maribel bit her lip. "I wish I wasn't in this situation. I wish my past was different."

Brian held her hand and squeezed it. "I am sure that whatever it is we can work it out. You can't base your future on your past."

He leaned forward and kissed her on her pink lips. The sensation was that of an electric charge.

He pulled back abruptly. "Wow."

Maribel gazed at him, a soft, unfocused look in her eyes. She touched her lips wonderingly. "Imagine if we actually really kissed."

Brian was still staring at her hungrily. She leaned forward and ran her tongue along his lips and he opened her mouth to hers. They hungrily kissed, a passionate embrace that was so explosive that for a moment Brian actually lost all thought as to the time of day or what was happening around them.

Brian reluctantly drew away from Maribel and tried hard not to stare at her pink lips and her dreamy expression. He had almost allowed passion to take over; never before in his life had he lost so much control. He tried to remember a Bible verse or two. He had to cool off; being in the car with her at this moment would derail all his convictions on sex before marriage. Never before had he been so tempted. He leapt out of the car and into the downpour outside.

They drove up to a mansion in Negril. The house was poised on a hill that seemed to be surrounded by the blue Caribbean Sea. The tension in the car was thick. Brian was thinking of the earth-shattering kiss and Maribel was tense because she had been to the house before.

She was flagellating herself mentally and she felt sick with worry. Why on earth did she agree to come back to the scene of the crime, as Brian had so unwittingly put it?

She grew up in the West End of Negril but she had naively thought she would not have met up on anybody that she had known. She had naively thought that with the passage of time and the reverting of herself to a more natural look, no one would readily recognize her, but here she was in the driveway of one of her biggest customers, Phillip Oliver Temple, attorney at law. When she had left Negril he had been planning to run as Member of Parliament for the area. He had been her regular Wednesday client, because that was the day his wife Valeria and daughter Ingrid went to the neighboring town of Savanna-la-mar for their weekly spa treatment.

An hour's drive away the two women would spend approximately six hours pampering themselves, while

Phillip lived out his wild fantasies with her and Felicia.

Maribel closed her eyes and wondered wildly if she was insane.

She hadn't asked Brian who his cousin was or where in Negril they were going. How could she be such an idiot? Her brain had surely been short-circuiting lately. There was no excuse for her stupidity. She barely glanced at the sprawling green lawns and the ornamental plants artfully scattered throughout the yard.

She was already familiar with Valeria's rose garden and the gazebo that was actually built above the sea.

She watched Brian as he stretched and then smiled at her. "This place is gorgeous, isn't it?"

Maribel froze. Would it look odd if she ran down the hill toward the wrought iron gates and ran off into the sunset, never looking back—running away from who she was then and who she was now?

"It's okay." She pinned a bright smile on her face. "I used to live in this town, remember?"

"You are looking positively panicked," Brian observed astutely. "I had no idea that Negril would have such a drastic effect on you. Your father can't get you here, Maribel."

Brian came to her side of the car and hugged her. "Now cheer up."

"Who is your cousin?" Maribel asked curiously. "Is it Ingrid that's getting married?"

Brian looked at her, shocked. "You know these people?"

Maribel shook her head. "Not really. I know of them."

"Oh," Brian smiled, "that's great. Uncle Phillip is my father's youngest brother."

"I didn't know he was a church man." Maribel swallowed. "I always thought he was a bit of a worldly man, if you know what I mean."

Brian laughed. "Uncle Phil is a church elder. What on earth gave you the idea that he was worldly?"

"Just some stuff I heard." Maribel cleared her throat. She didn't want to go inside, so she stalled some more, forcing Brian, who was in the process of getting their bags from the car, to pause.

"So how come his name is Temple?" Maribel asked curiously.

Brian smiled. "He was my grandmother's only child with her second husband."

"Oh," Maribel said, "I didn't know your grandmother had another husband after your grandfather."

"Yes she did." Brian held her hand. "Let's go. He is still alive; you'll get to meet him. I am so happy that you are getting to meet some of my family members now. I can't wait until you meet Mom and Dad and my sisters, but those people inside are some of my closest family members in Jamaica."

Maribel winced. She had already met his uncle in the most intimate of ways and she wished that she never had to meet him again. This cemented in her mind that she had to say no to Brian's proposal tonight. When they were heading for Kingston she would just break up with him, get it over and done with. It would be utterly humiliating to tell the man that you love, "Oh by the way, I had sex with your uncle every Wednesday for close to two years. He was my highest paying customer."

The house was bustling with activity. The security guard at the gate had radioed up to the house that they were coming and Valeria had waited in the front foyer for them. She was arranging pink and white roses in red stained pots when they walked through. The house was just as Maribel remembered it: huge and expensive, with marble floor tiles and a central wall made of cut stone in a faded, soft brown, leading into the spacious kitchen.

Maribel looked at Valeria in the flesh for the first time and had to stop herself from staring. She was shorter than her pictures had suggested, her coffee-colored skin was unlined and her teeth were blindingly white.

"My baby," she exclaimed when she saw Brian. "I can't believe you came to Jamaica to work and they sent you to Kingston, of all places. We rarely see you."

She hugged Brian tightly and then looked over at Maribel. "And who is this?"

"Maribel," Brian said proudly, "this is my aunt Valeria."

"Hello," Valeria said, hugging Maribel. "You are very welcome here."

"Thank you," Maribel said, smiling.

"Where is Uncle Phil?" Brian asked excitedly. "And the bride to be?"

"Phil is in his study, trying to pretend that the house is not in chaos. Ingrid is in her room crying because one of her bridesmaids can't make it to the wedding."

"That's sad," Maribel said, wishing that she had not put foot in the house and wishing that she had not met Valeria and saw that she was such a nice person.

"It might not be, now that you are here," Valeria said cheekily. "You are about the same size as Crystal, the missing bridesmaid."

"But ... but ... " Maribel stumbled; she couldn't participate in the wedding. She was already having heart palpitations at the ordeal of meeting Phillip and now she would be participating in his daughter's wedding. *How bad can this get, Lord? How bad?*

"Do a quick visit with your uncle," Valeria said, ignoring

Maribel's protest. "I will fetch Maribel in a while."

Brian grinned at Maribel and said, "Isn't it cool? You can practice for our wedding."

"I didn't say yes."

"But she didn't say no either," he said to his aunt, who was looking as pleased as can be.

They headed toward the study and Maribel found herself dragging her feet the nearer they came to the door.

"Come on," Brian laughed, "he won't bite."

He knocked and Phillip gruffly said, "Enter ... if you are not going to ask me wedding-related questions."

Brian opened the door and laughed, "Uncle Phil."

Phillip stood up when Brian entered. He was a tall man with graying side burns. His face was ruggedly handsome—tennis and jogging kept him looking fit. He greeted Brian with a hug and patted him on the back. Maribel hesitated at the door. He hadn't seen her yet and she was hovering at the door, trying to delay the inevitable.

"So how are you" Phillip was walking toward the door, "and who do we have out here?"

He flung the door wider and his face froze in shock. His eyes ran up and down Maribel slowly and then rested on her face. "Peaches?"

"No Uncle, that's Maribel," Brian said behind his uncle. "She is the lady that I asked to marry me."

Phillip swallowed and then swung around to Brian. "Okay ..." He cleared his throat. "Come on in, Maribel. Pleased to meet you." He shook her hand.

"Hello Phillip," Maribel said quietly.

She squirmed as the atmosphere in the study became thick with tension.

"So," Phillip released Maribel's hand and sat in one of the chairs that was in the office, "have a seat—have a seat."

Brian could sense that something was not right; Maribel was holding herself so stiffly that he suspected that if he poked her she would shatter like glass. His uncle had a sheepish look on his face, as if he was recovering from a shock, and what was that about him calling Maribel Peaches?

He didn't get to explore the scenario further because Ingrid had burst into the study; she was in a diaphanous robe with a blue silk pajama. Her hair was in fine curlers and her eyes looked puffy.

"Oh Brian, I am so happy to see you," she sniffed, "and this is Maribel?"

Maribel nodded, relieved; she had been on tenterhooks when she realized that Phillip had recognized her. She was just waiting for the guillotine to chop off her head when Ingrid made her grand entrance with an aura of desperation about her.

"Thank God, you are so pretty, and just the right size," she was babbling. "The Lord does answer prayers. Would you mind being my bridesmaid? Your hair is the right length for the curls. Thank God. Did you say yes? Let's go upstairs."

She grabbed Maribel's hand and ushered her out of the room. Maribel looked back at Brian helplessly.

"I hope you like burnt orange because that is my wedding color. My name is Ingrid, by the way, and I am Brian's favorite cousin. I am marrying Dean—he is so dreamy. I've known him since he was ten. I can't believe that I am marrying him today."

She talked on and on, and Maribel could not get a word in edgewise.

"Why did you call her Peaches?" Brian asked his uncle when the women left.

"Do you want a drink?" Phillip asked, stalling; he couldn't

tell Brian the truth without exposing himself and yet he was appalled that Peaches was here in his house again. He had searched Negril for her when she disappeared and now here she was in his house, engaged to his nephew.

"No thanks," Brian said impatiently. "Why did you call Maribel Peaches?"

"Because that's her pet name," Phillip said reluctantly. "I've known her since she was a very young girl."

Phillip stressed the very young trying to deflect Brian from his suspicions. Whatever they were.

"Oh," Brian relaxed. "Where do you know her from? She did say that she was from Negril and had a rotten childhood."

"Ah," Phillip relaxed in his chair with a drink in hand, "she used to do some work for me. I tried to help her out, you know."

Brian nodded, relieved. For just a minute there he had wondered briefly if Maribel had had a relationship with his uncle. The thought made him cringe. How could he think such nonsense? He needed to ask the Lord to purify his thoughts. But just for a minute, when the tension had built to boiling point, he had thought that his uncle had known Maribel on an intimate level.

He switched the conversation but the sensation of being left in the dark came roaring back incessantly. How was it that Maribel said she only knew of his family and now his uncle said that she had worked for him? He vowed that he would find out once and for all whatever it was that was so bad in Maribel's past.

Chapter Sixteen

"**D**o you really have to go to Kingston tonight?" Ingrid hugged Maribel. "You could use my old bedroom and Brian can sleep in the guest room."

"It is late, but I have work tomorrow," Maribel said, smiling. No way in hell would she be staying in Phillip Temple's house tonight. He was staring at her all day, a puppy dog look on his face. He made several attempts to talk to her but Ingrid was like a drill sergeant with her eight bridesmaids. They were constantly on the move.

"Time to go." Brian appeared at her elbow. He seemed a little pensive and Maribel looked at him warily.

"Oh, okay … it was a great wedding, Ingrid. I loved it."

"Thank you. Brian, I will return the favor as a bridesmaid at your wedding when you two get married," Ingrid gushed.

Maribel looked at the way that he hesitated before answering and felt a little niggle of fright enter her thoughts. Did Phillip say something to him? Of course he wouldn't; he would not want his nephew to know that he had a habit of using prostitutes when his wife was away. She was counting on him having too much to lose to spill the beans on her.

She moved away from Brian and Ingrid and headed toward the car. The place was packed but she knew just where Brian had parked. She had already said her goodbyes to Valeria—a guilty shaft had pierced her as she thought about what she used to do behind the lady's back with her husband, but that was her unconverted self, she kept reminding herself.

Phillip was at the car when she approached it; she thought that she had lost him in the crowd.

"I know I don't have to tell you not to say a word about our previous association," Phillip said. He was standing in the last glare of the sunset.

Maribel frowned. "What association?"

"Good girl," Phillip clapped. "You can't join the family, Peaches." Phillip leaned on the car and crossed his arms. "You are a whore; Brian is a pastor."

Maribel winced. "I was a whore. Not anymore."

"Your body has been through so many men."

"Including you," Maribel retorted. "So just shut up and stop this stupid double standard. I was shocked to hear that you are a church elder. At least when I used to sell my body, I had no knowledge of God and his goodness. I had no spouse and child. You are such a hypocrite in so many ways; you sinned against God and your marriage." She was breathing hard.

Phillip straightened up. "For a man it's different."

"That's crap." Maribel snorted. "You are as much a whore as I used to be. Because you are the one paying doesn't make you less of a whore. As far as I know, all sin is sin in God's eyes."

"Nice speech," Phillip said angrily, "but I don't want you

in my family."

"I don't care what you want," Maribel retorted. "It's up to Brian what he wants."

"That's because Brian doesn't know what a mess he would be embroiling himself in with you."

"You don't know me," Maribel stressed angrily. "Brian knows the true me. All you knew was a girl who used to flatter your ego and give you sexual release."

Phillip laughed. "Is that so, Peaches? Are you forgetting the days when you used to cry to me about your rotten childhood and when I used to hold you when you complained about that fat, slimy landlord whose equivalent of rent collecting was a blowjob?"

Maribel closed her eyes.

"That's right," Phillip said angrily, "I am the one who paid those Jamrotic guys back their money after Cream ran off with it. I made them know that they were never to mess with you because you were innocent. They shot her anyway. I made it known that you were not to be touched. In essence, Peaches, I am your benefactor. The man who made it possible for you to be the prim and proper church-going Maribel. But I did not expect that you would be making plans to marry my nephew. Do me a favor and stay away from him. The man deserves better than you for a wife."

Maribel swallowed; tears were seeping unchecked along her cheeks. She didn't even recognize when Phillip moved in front of her and brushed her cheeks. "I still want you. I can set you up in a nice house near here and you and I can still have what we had. What we had was more than you are trying to lower it to. Except this time, I want exclusivity; no one else for you but me. I used to hate it when I saw you only on Wednesdays. I used to hate that with a passion."

Maribel moved away blindly and ran into Brian, who was

coming toward the car.

"Hey Maribel," he caught her hand and drew her to him in an embrace, "what's wrong?"

Maribel cried and hiccupped, "It's all falling apart."

Brian hugged her to him and inhaled her scent; it was a flowery mix of jasmine and citrus.

He rubbed her back and marveled at her shapely form. "Hush now, let's get ourselves on the road, and stop somewhere and talk."

Maribel nodded in his neck. "I am sorry, Brian. I am so sorry you met me."

Brian kissed the top of her head. "I am happy I met you, Maribel, so happy. I can't find Uncle Phil anywhere. I wanted to tell him goodbye."

"Let's not," Maribel shuddered.

"Okay." Brian let her into the car and came around to his side contemplatively. "Were you just talking to him?"

"Yes," Maribel mumbled.

"You two had a sexual relationship, didn't you?"

Maribel sniffled.

"Oh Maribel," Brian sighed. "I am going to assume that the answer is yes."

Maribel quietly sobbed in her side of the car as Brian drove off.

"I am not mad," he said to Maribel quietly. "I suspected that something was not quite right when we were in the study. I am just taken aback—confused, but not very surprised though. You keep on warning me that you have a past. I keep on skirting the issue because I am not sure that I am ready for the details. I want to know more and it might be that it may not be so good for me, you know. Was this why you can't marry me?"

Maribel considered taking the easy way out and saying yes

and then she remembered that Thelma was out there, a loose cannon.

"There's more." Her nose was all stuffed up and her voice sounded hoarse.

Brian sighed. "Can I process this one for a while, please?" Maribel nodded.

They drove in silence as Brian thought about it. So she had an affair with his married uncle. He could live with that; she obviously did it when she was young. She did not have a father figure in her life; she was a young girl in Negril without proper guidance or any Christian connection. He could forgive that. He was writing a book on forgiveness, for God's sake; in the whole scheme of things, what she did was negligible.

There was more, she had said; well, he would just have to wait to hear what more. He was still trying to wrap his mind around the fact that his uncle was not the upstanding pillar of Christianity that he had thought he was.

She got an email the Monday morning after the fateful Sunday night. She had cried herself into exhaustion and Brian had not pressed her for more information. He had spoken about his book and his family in Canada—everything but Maribel's past.

When he dropped her home after ten o'clock she felt as if she had run a marathon. In the morning she got an email from him. "We didn't celebrate your birthday the way we should have on Sunday. Happy belated birthday. Can we do it on Wednesday instead?"

She had written back that Wednesday was fine.

Wednesday was as good a day as any to give a full confession.

"How did it go?" Vivian stuck her head around the door.

"I'll tell you at lunch," Maribel said wearily. "I am in the mood to go home and sleep for the rest of the week. I hate Mondays."

"I hate that portfolio you are supposed to give me." Vivian came into the office fully. "It is complicated."

"Hence the reason why Maribel has it," Mark said, opening the door wider and entering after Vivian.

Maribel jumped.

"I am not eavesdropping," he declared importantly, "just here to announce that we got the Lawrence account, lock, stock and barrel. You, Miss Contrell, will be the proud head of that portfolio, and you, Miss Reid," he looked at Vivian, "will be the head of Hodges Construction."

"The two of you, I need to meet in my office at twelve today. It's a long meeting so you might want to bring your lunch."

Vivian looked at Maribel when Mark walked out of the office. "So much for the tell-all at lunch. But did you tell Brian?"

"No," Maribel groaned, "not yet. I am thinking Wednesday."

"Well, Happy belated birthday. I have a day trip to the spa for two." She pulled out the gift vouchers from her bag. "One for me and one for you."

"Thank you." Maribel got up and hugged her. "You are a good friend."

Vivian grinned. "Of course I am, and because I am your best friend I am getting one of those tickets."

Maribel laughed. "I would rather go with you than anyone else."

There was going to be a thunderstorm on Wednesday. Maribel was feeling as gray and dull as the clouds outside.

She had psyched herself up to tell Brian and now she felt a little faint and a great deal nervous.

He had said he'd come over at five-thirty and she waited like a cat on hot bricks.

Brian was excited, though he had not quite gotten over the thought of Maribel and his uncle together. His opinion of Maribel as an innocent Christian lady had been shattered but there was so much more to her than who she had had sex with.

This evening was the evening when they would start afresh. He would reassure her that her past did not matter that much to him, and that he wanted to marry her anyway. He had even vowed to himself that he would have to keep his uncle and Maribel apart at future family get-togethers.

His family were huge fans of family gatherings, so that was something he knew he would have to deal with if he got married to Maribel. His father was the quintessential family man, who was always eager to host a family party.

His stomach twisted when he thought of his father; he was not doing well. His mother, being the alarmist that she was, had convinced him that his father was on his deathbed. Though his father had adamantly told Brian that he was doing well, he was anxious to see him.

Every day Pastor Green called him, his voice sounding like sandpaper on wood, demanding to find out if Brian wanted to switch back so that he could escape the cold. The truth was, he was getting very fond of the members at United Church and he was in no haste to go back to Canada, except to see his father.

If Maribel said yes, he would have to stay for a while for them to get married and sort themselves out. If she said no— he didn't want to think of that. Life would be so much easier if she said yes.

He parked his car in a visitor's parking space and anticipated the moment when he would see her sweet face. She was such a beautiful woman.

His cellular phone rang and he answered it before getting out of the car.

"Oh Pastor Brian, I am so happy I caught you."

"Hello Sister Thelma," Brian answered with a smile on his face. She was always calling him about something trivial or to brag about Rose.

"I went to Negril the other day, as you know."

"Did you have a great time?" Brian asked while locking the car door.

"Oh yes," Thelma gushed, "I learnt a lot."

"Well, that's good." Brian switched the phone to his other ear and headed toward Maribel's second floor apartment.

"I was very interested in a porn star duo called Peaches and Cream," Thelma said, her voice still sounding high-pitched and sweet, "so I dragged Horace to Negril to find out more."

"Porn, as in pornography?" Brian asked incredulously.

"Oh yes," Thelma said. "I found out that they were first prostitutes on the road, selling their bodies mainly to tourists, and then they did a whopping fourteen porn videos, most of them together, with some shocking lesbian scenes."

"Why are you telling me this?" Brian asked, exasperated. He was nearing Maribel's door and was ready to cut off Thelma.

"Because ..." Thelma said, anticipation thickening her voice, "our Sister Maribel is Peaches, and her friend Felicia was Cream. I was shocked, I tell you, pastor, that such a nice young lady was a common prostitute. Not that there is anything uncommon about prostitution."

"Run that by me again?" Brian paused before he pressed the buzzer above Maribel's door. Hadn't his uncle called her Peaches? He felt a ringing in his ear and he had to lean against the wall. Could it be true? Was Maribel a prostitute?

"Shocking, isn't it?" Thelma was saying shrilly in the phone. "I could see her doing the porn videos, but as I'm told—from some very shady sources, I should add—she used to sell her body for a measly $500 per night. I shudder to think of all the slimy men that have …"

Brian exhaled, "Sister Thelma, could you keep this to yourself? I have to go now. I will talk to you later."

"Oh sure." Thelma had gentled her voice to a purr. "Sure."

Chapter Seventeen

He pressed the buzzer anyway, a decision he was not sure that he should have made after hearing such shattering news. He wanted to ask her about it. Hell, he wanted to laugh about it with her and tell her to sue Thelma for slander, but something inside him, that intuition which he prided himself on, was telling him that Thelma was telling the truth.

That was the major secret that Maribel was withholding. He studied the door panels fiercely; he actually felt numb.

She opened the door. She was in a pink dress and she smelled so good. He walked in the apartment and sat on a settee and stared into space. His brain ran over and over lurid scenes that sickened him to think about. This was beyond the pale. This was …

"Are you okay, Brian?" Maribel was looking at him, concerned.

He looked at her fully for the first time in his life, with all the scales dropped off from his eyes, and all he saw was the same beautiful, gentle woman he fell in love with. Thelma was just winding him up. She must have been crazy to tell him such a whopping lie about the woman he loved.

"Maribel?" Brian asked warily.

Maribel stiffened uncomfortably; he had a shattered look in his eye, as if something terrible had happened.

"Were you a prostitute?"

Maribel sat frozen in her chair. *How did he find out?* she asked herself. *It must have been Thelma and her infernal investigation.*

"I sit here and I look at you and I think, this must be a crazy question but you are just sitting there and I am thinking, no God, this can't be right. She's not laughing, she's not denying it."

"Brian, that's … that's … what I wanted to talk to you about." Maribel clutched her shaking hands in her lap. "My story is not a pretty one. Just hear me out, please."

Brian closed his eyes and swallowed. A lump had formed in his chest, a fist in his stomach and a hammer in his head. He could feel tears forming below his eyelids and he willed them not to fall. He felt amazingly let down. He felt as if he was dropped from a twenty-story building head first into concrete. "Brian?" Maribel questioned uncertainly.

"I am listening," Brian said hoarsely.

"I ran away from home at seventeen," Maribel said tremulously. "I ran straight into the car of a man I did not know." She swallowed. "I lived with him for three months, till his wife kicked me out. I had to survive somehow, so I met this girl Felicia who was very street smart at the time, and she told me we could make money as nude models."

Maribel could hear the clock ticking in the kitchen. The room was so quiet she didn't even know if Brian was still breathing. He had his hands clenched together and his eyes closed.

"When we went to the place where we were supposed to model, they asked us to do some videos. We drank and took drugs, and I to this day can't recall half the things I did. In a two-month period I did about fourteen pornographic videos. The guys refused to pay us and Felicia decided to help herself to a bag of US money that she found. When she ran away I ran with her and we set up shop in a hole-in-the-wall place in Negril. We started doing high class hooking with people like your uncle. It paid the bills and fed our party lifestyle. And then two years later, I gave it up when Felicia died; went to live with a guy who was willing to keep me and started dancing for a living at different street dances. Felicia was shot at a party because of the money she stole. Ironically, it was money that she did not even use. She had hidden it in an account. That's the money I used to escape Negril."

Maribel bit her lip and stared at Brian. He hadn't moved since she started telling her story.

"Do you even have any idea how many men you have had sex with?" Brian asked incredulously, opening one bloodshot eye to look at her.

Maribel frowned. "No, I don't."

Brian heaved a sigh. "Is there anything else? Have you murdered anyone? Had several abortions? Have a disease? Tell me; I want to know."

Maribel sighed. A hysterical giggle was forming in her throat. "No, I haven't murdered anyone, nor do I have a disease, nor have I had any abortions."

"Do you still do drugs?" Brian asked, looking at her with pain stamped on his features.

"No." Maribel frowned; she had vowed that she would not cry. She wouldn't, at least not today. She had done all her crying already. A tear escaped her eye and she wiped it away fiercely. "I haven't done drugs since I was nineteen. Haven't had a drink since I joined the church."

"Are you bisexual?" He suddenly remembered Thelma telling him about her lesbian scenes.

Maribel shook her head. "No I just did it for the money. Those kind of things copped a higher price—the kinkier, the better."

Maribel suddenly felt lighter now that she had told him. now there was no secret between them. It was all out there for him to see now. She didn't have to worry about keeping such a huge secret from him anymore. The ball was now squarely in his court.

Brian rubbed his temples slowly; there was a dull ache behind his eyes. This was really an explosive moment for him, "Maribel this is deep." His voice was rough. "I just barely wrapped my mind around the fact that you slept with my uncle and now this bombshell. This is a big deal.

"I don't want to respond to what you just told me with scorn or disdain; that would not be God's way and I really am trying to be like Jesus but the man ... the man in me is recoiling.

"The man that wanted a pure bride, or at least one that didn't have a tainted history as huge as yours, is screaming to just get up and go. And still there is another part of me that wants to know, how could you? Couldn't you have gone to some women's shelter? Visited a church? Gone to a children's home until you were eighteen? Learned a skill? Done legitimate work?

"Maribel, there are women who have been in your position or worse who would never have prostituted themselves. How could you allow strange men to ... even my own uncle? I have to get out of here." Brian stood up.

He pushed his hand into his jacket pocket and felt the

engagement ring he had bought for her and had fully expected to give her tonight. He couldn't give it to her now, if ever.

He looked at her and grimaced. "I am sorry, Maribel, I need time to process all this."

She nodded—her lips were trembling.

He wondered how many men had felt those lips on various body parts, and that thought alone had him marching to the door in blind fury.

Would he ever see her the same way again? She had broken something within him that he didn't know if he could get back. Many things were coming clear to him now: the taunts about peaches and cream that Thelma made the other night, the reluctance of Maribel to get close to him and tell him her past.

That earth-shattering kiss they shared on Sunday—how much of that was experience from an ex-whore or just genuine passion? He braced himself on the doorjamb after he swung the door open. His mind was ticking a mile a minute.

"I'll probably call you. I can't think right now."

She didn't answer. She just stared at his back in mute pain and that, more than anything, made him angrier with himself and angrier at her.

Chapter Eighteen

Maribel called in to work sick the next day. Her voice was so hoarse from crying that Annabelle from Human Resources had hurriedly gotten her off the phone and admonished her to see a doctor. But Maribel knew that her problem could not be helped by any doctor. In the last few months, her life had spiraled out of control. Her relatively quiet post-Negril days were now over.

She was forced to battle Mark, confide in Vivian, she had met up with Phillip at his daughter's wedding and then the ultimate worst thing had happened—she had loved and lost the most caring man in the whole world.

Her eyes were partially swollen and her tear ducts were dry. She huddled in the bed and tried to think positive thoughts, but all of Friday passed in a blur.

She didn't answer the doorbell or her cell phone. She didn't care. As far as she knew her life was over. When Thelma told Horace, if she hadn't done so already, he would probably pull their account from her company and would probably tell Mark why he no longer wanted to do business with them. The fallout from that would be too humiliating to consider.

Then there would be church. It was hard to be a sinner at church, or at least lay your sins bare for all the brethren to see.

It was night outside when she thought of the fallout from church. Some people would treat her as if she had some contagious disease; others would probably find it very hard not to be gleeful about her situation. She was pretty sure she would not be going back to that church.

It would be too much to hope that Thelma would keep her mouth shut and not broadcast what she had learned and allow Maribel a modicum of peace in her life.

A dull pounding at her door had her dragging herself out of the bed and staggering in the hallway. The pounding had gone on for close to ten minutes and Maribel could not ignore it anymore.

She peeped through the keyhole and saw Cathy and Vivian, looking concerned as they took turns knocking. She opened the door in Vivian's mid-knock and was almost knocked sideways when Vivian fell on her and hugged her.

"Thank God, I was going to get the police, I swear, if you hadn't opened the door."

Cathy pushed Vivian aside and said, "Let me get a hug; I've been so worried. Vivian said you called in sick and that you had some major issues going on and that you wouldn't answer your phone."

Maribel sighed and stepped aside. "Come in." She shuffled toward her living area and fell in a settee with her legs dangling off. "I feel like an old woman who hasn't been taking her calcium. Can you hear my bones creaking?"

Vivian sat across from her, looking concerned. "So what's

wrong? Why are your eyes so swollen? You look as if you have been crying."

Maribel looked at Cathy contemplatively. "Cathy, this may come as a shock to you. I told Viv already, so she shouldn't be too shocked. I was a prostitute, starred in a couple of porn videos. Et cetera, et cetera. Blah, blah, blah." She threw her hands up in the air.

Cathy half smiled. "You told me that one night when you came in drunk from a party while we were in college. I never pressed you about it; I figured if you wanted to tell me when you were sober you would."

Maribel opened her eyes wider. "All this time you knew."

Cathy nodded. "Yes, and yet we are still friends. It doesn't change anything for me. I must confess I was a bit shocked when I heard—you were going on and on about how beastly your life was, and I just let you talk."

Maribel shook her head. "I can't believe I just freely spoke about it like that."

Vivian stood up. "She told me the other day and I was shocked. I encouraged her to tell Brian since he proposed."

"He did what?" Cathy jumped up and down on the settee. "You are going to marry Pastor Handsome and you did not see it fit to tell me?"

"I was uncertain, ashamed about my past, very restless in my spirit. I wondered if I should tell him or not, but it so happens that I didn't even get the chance. It seems as if Thelma did."

"So how did he take it?" Vivian, who was on her way to the kitchen, turned back.

"He was very distraught." Maribel sniffed, remembering the look in Brian's eyes. "I don't think he will ever talk to me again. He couldn't bear to look at me after."

Cathy nodded. "I guess that reaction can be expected for

now."

Vivian sighed. "Well, it's better that its all out in the open."

Maribel looked at both of her friends and smiled. "I spent all day in bed feeling sorry for myself, even imagining that I was back at square one where my life was concerned. My job is on the line, my relationship is in the trash can, but I am just now remembering that I have several blessings. I still have you guys."

Cathy got up and hugged her. "And you always will my dear."

Later, after they had talked and laughed way up into the night and Maribel was alone again, she felt more like her old self and was able to look at things philosophically. She picked up her Bible for the comfort she would find in it.

After all, didn't God say that we should come boldly to the throne of grace? Besides, what could she do about her past? It was already gone. She regretted everything that she had done, but really, there was no use in flagellating herself over the same thing over and over. God said he was faithful and just to forgive and she believed him, so her past was forgiven. She just needed to forgive herself and move on.

She felt better after praying and closed her eyes as she thought about Brian. What was he doing now? How was he feeling about her? She turned on her side and caressed her pillow. Would she ever have the opportunity to have a husband she could turn to in the lonely hours of the night and talk, or had she forfeited all of that with her youthful mistakes?

She closed her eyes and in her mind's eye could see Brian as they walked together on their regular walking trail, his face suffused with the joy of being with her. Would she ever see those brown eyes smiling her way again? A lone tear trickled down the side of her face. She was going to stop thinking about Brian for now. Obviously that was still a bleeding wound.

Maribel had packed her weekend bag and headed for the Goblin Hill Guest House in Portland for a full week. She had informed her friends and her workplace and then turned off her phone. The time away in the quiet parish, with its tranquil blue sea and lush green vegetation, was good for her. She had idled away her time in a hammock overlooking the sea and read detective novels.

She had Dido's *White Flag* constantly playing on her iPod and it brought a tear or two to her eyes. The guesthouse staff left her alone as she wallowed in her pity fest and came to terms with her loss.

It was not a shock to her when she turned on her phone after driving back from Portland and found that she had a gazillion missed calls from Thelma Lawrence. She contemplated calling her back but decided that she was going to ignore her for the time being.

It was, however, a great shock when she pulled up outside her apartment building and saw Horace Lawrence waiting for her.

He got out of his car when he saw her driving in and waited patiently as she locked her car door and faced him warily. "I saw a whopping 97 missed calls from your wife."

Horace grinned and scratched his beard. "She was not too comfortable with you disappearing on her. You weren't around for her to gloat and she started getting worried."

Maribel nodded. "So are you here to deliver the news that you cannot have me handling your firm's account?"

Horace smiled. "Thelma would have wanted that; actually, she suggested it, but I vetoed her on that one. Your friend Vivian told me that you were coming in today. Luckily, I did not have to wait too long for you to get here. I just stopped by to tell you that everyone has a past, some more colorful than others, but if you dig deep enough there is something in everyone's background that they would rather keep quiet. Take Thelma, for example."

Maribel straightened up; she couldn't believe what she was hearing. Horace was on her side.

"Thelma?" Maribel whispered hoarsely, tensing up slightly. She wanted to drag the words from Horace's mouth.

"Well … my … delightful wife was not always the paragon of saintliness that you see in church. She doesn't know that I know that Rose is not my child."

Maribel's mouth hung open.

Horace laughed, "Shocking, isn't it?"

She nodded mutely.

"Rose is my business partner's child. She had an affair with him when I was abroad doing my doctorate. At the time, she passed off Rose as a premature baby, but my partner confessed about the affair to me. To this day I haven't said a thing to Thelma. Your fate is now in Thelma's hands; I just thought you should go into the fight with a little ammo. I am just telling you this to make a point that nobody is perfect. Hell, I am not perfect. You have done a great job for my company so far; keep at it. I wish you all the best with your pastor."

Maribel nodded. "Thank you so much. I doubt he will be able to look past what I used to do, you know …"

Horace shrugged. "These days I am not so hung up on judging people. I think God was clearly instructing us when he said judgment is His, don't you think?"

"Oh yes," Maribel whispered fervently, "and he is still in the prayer-answering business apparently. I specifically told him to take care of this situation for me."

"There you go." Horace got into his car. "Take care."

He tooted his horn and drove out of the complex, leaving a very stunned Maribel behind. *He told me Thelma's secret so that we would be even.* She just couldn't believe it. This really was a miracle.

Chapter Nineteen

Church was packed the next Sabbath when Maribel drove into the parking lot; she entered the foyer with tense anticipation and collected a program from one of the ushers.

"Oh Sister Maribel." Carlene rushed up to her, her round face beaming. "I have not seen you at Women's Ministries Meeting now for two weeks."

Maribel smiled, "I've been a bit busy these past couple of Sundays."

"Well, I announced last week that I am engaged."

Maribel gasped. "You are? To who? Let me see the ring."

"He doesn't believe in jewelry wearing," Carlene giggled.

"Or women talking in church," Cathy sidled up to the two of them and kissed Maribel on the cheek.

"He is just a bit eccentric." Carlene's ears were bright red.

"He is plain weird," Cathy laughed. "Do you remember Brother Timble, the man who sits at the back of church and plays the mouth organ and has five-six kids? His wife died four months ago and Carlene here is her replacement."

"Well, I asked the Lord for a husband," Carlene said, frowning, "and he answered my prayers."

"Do me a favor," Cathy whispered as people were coming toward them, "and wait on the Lord and stop jumping up and down to get married. Virginity has never killed anybody yet, and I am sure it won't kill you. Can you really imagine lying beside Brother Timble night after night while he humps you energetically while playing his mouth organ?"

Carlene gasped, "Cathy, this is the house of the Lord."

"And God created sex," Cathy said, grinning. "He wants us to enjoy it with our spouse, not lie down and think of Beulah Land."

Carlene eyes widened like saucers. "Brother Timble says I should not consider what goes on between a man and a woman outside of a bedroom."

Cathy rolled her eyes. "Brother Timble? You are actually calling your future husband Brother Timble? Lord have mercy, please get counseling before you marry Bertram Timble, and get him to fix his front teeth before you march down the aisle in your wedding finery."

Maribel shuddered in mirth as Cathy laid it on Carlene.

Carlene looked wounded and said a limp goodbye to Maribel, while she pointedly ignored Cathy.

"Cathy, you are something else." Maribel searched her purse for a kerchief to wipe her eyes. "Do you think Carlene is that desperate for a man?"

Cathy snorted, "Someone has to tell her the truth. Brother Timble is looking for a housemaid and a doormat. On a brighter note, I am happy to see you in church today. I was planning to come and haul you out of your apartment if I didn't see you but here you are, fresh as a daisy and looking spiffy in that red suit."

Maribel smiled. "Thanks."

"I thought you would have been cowering in fear from Sister Thelma and her busybody tongue."

Maribel grinned. "Let's just say that Sister Thelma and I are on a level playing field, and her husband says he is quite pleased with my work and won't be telling my boss a thing. As a matter of fact, I can't wait to see Thelma."

Cathy giggled, "Go girl, stick it to her."

Maribel was about to reply when she saw Brian enter the foyer. He was talking to an elder. As if he sensed her presence he looked up, and their eyes met and held. For a split second Maribel felt her heart racing like a car on a steep hill without brakes. And like the metaphorical car, her heart raced out of control and was heading for a precipice when he walked over and said, "Hello Maribel, Cathy."

"Pastor Edwards," Cathy said formally.

Maribel gave him a tremulous half smile. She looked in his eyes to see if there was anything in them for her, but they were shuttered. He looked tired and sad. She hastily turned away when the elder grabbed his attention again, and they headed into the church.

"That was intense," Cathy murmured beside her.

Maribel tucked her trembling hands through her friend's and walked shakily into church.

"The topic of today's sermon is forgiveness." Brian looked out at the congregation; he had planned to preach this sermon since he first came to the church but he hadn't gotten the chance, but now, today of all the days, the moment when he was least sure of himself, he was preaching on the topic.

Ever since Maribel had gutted him with her news he was

not so sure that forgiveness was such an easy thing to do. Even after praying about it and wrestling with it, he still felt a burning ache in his gut when he thought about her past. He just couldn't get past it. It made him angry and vulnerable. He took turns wanting to kill her parents for such a rotten childhood and then praying that the Lord forgive him for his thoughts and then wanting to shake Maribel and ask her why she had to succumb to such a depraved lifestyle.

He glanced over at her in her red dress and fluffy hairstyle, looking as innocent as the first day he met her, and knew why he was waffling so much. He had this sermon that he was reluctant to preach because he was doing the very opposite of the words laid out on the paper in front of him. He was, quite frankly, not practicing what he was about to preach, and this made him edgy and uncomfortable.

"Brothers and Sisters," he cleared his throat, "as most of you know I am writing a book on forgiveness. When I started writing the book I thought that it would be fun to research and explore the limits to which human beings will go to forgive their fellow men. You see, brethren, it is very easy to talk about this thing called forgiveness, but it is entirely another matter to do it. What is very scary about forgiveness is that without it the Lord does not answer our prayers. Don't believe me? Turn your Bibles to Matthew 6; here Jesus taught his disciples how to pray.

"Embedded in that prayer is the whole issue of forgiveness. While we are asking for forgiveness we should also forgive. Jesus himself said, 'For if you forgive men their trespasses your heavenly father will also forgive you.' But if we don't forgive, then there is no forgiveness for us. It is as simple and as serious as that …"

Maribel listened to his voice and her eyes watered slightly.

Did this mean that he had forgiven her? Surely he wouldn't be up there preaching about forgiveness if he hadn't forgiven her.

She sighed. Forgiving and forgetting were two different sides of the coin. And he possibly needed a lot of time to forget her past. Maybe the next fifty years would suffice.

Or maybe he would have sudden acute amnesia and wouldn't remember anything that he learnt for the last week. She shook her head from her fanciful musings and glanced across at Thelma, who was sitting piously in a row across from hers, her broad black and white hat obscuring her face from view. Thelma had deliberately set out to reveal her life for everyone to see, just because she wanted the pastor for her precious Rose.

Rose had smiled at her earlier, an easy natural smile that gave Maribel no clue as to what her mother had said to her about her past. She couldn't wait to talk to Thelma so that she could ascertain how many persons were privy to the story of her past life.

She got her chance when standing beside her car and waving goodbye to Cathy and Greg. Thelma walked up to her and huffed, "I never thought I would see you around here again."

Maribel smiled. "Why not?"

"Because you are ... were ... a slut, a common whore. I told the pastor about your very crowded history and he seemed shocked."

"Well, church is a hospital for sinners. We all come here so that we can encourage each other along the way as we strive to go to heaven."

Thelma snorted, "For a prostitute you have a bold tongue."

"How many people have you told that I was a prostitute, Thelma?"

"I was ready to shout it to the world but the pastor came to my house and begged me not to," Thelma sniffed, "and Horace has gotten all cold and judgmental on me, as if I had done something wrong, so I will keep it under wraps for now. But don't expect me to after this—with your very cocky attitude."

"How do you want me to act?" Maribel questioned, folding her arms. "Beaten, scared, beholden to you?"

"You sold your body to numerous men; you have no right to be even standing there now looking at me, a decent person. Your type makes me sick. And then you have the nerve to come into this church and try to steal the attention of our pastor."

Maribel laughed. "*Your* type makes *me* sick." She sobered up and looked at Thelma seriously. "You are a hypocrite without a case. If you are so much better than me, Thelma, tell me, who is Rose's real father?"

Thelma gasped, "What did you say?"

"You heard me." Maribel looked out at the parking lot and waved to Sister Bertram.

She then glanced back at Thelma, who looked as if she was struggling for breath. "Here's the deal, Thelma: I am going to take the pastor's sermon to heart and I am going to forgive you your trespasses, and I fully expect you to forgive mine."

"Where did you ... how did you?" Thelma was tongue-tied and sounded garbled.

"Promise me you will shut your big, hypocritical mouth and I will promise you the same," Maribel said, looking at Thelma, a half smile playing along her lips.

"He won't marry you after this," Thelma sputtered.

"Promise me, Thelma," Maribel said strongly.

"Oh well, I promise. How did you find out about Rose? Nobody knows about that."

"About what?" Maribel asked innocently.

"About the little issue of her paternity."

"I don't know what you are talking about," Maribel said, a deadpan expression on her face. "You have a nice Sabbath now, Sister Thelma."

Thelma nodded and stepped away.

Maribel went into her car and pushed in her gospel CD. *The Lord's Prayer* by Aaron Neville filled the car with its soothing sound and she drove away, leaving a very deflated-looking Thelma in the parking lot.

Chapter Twenty

The song *Warning Sign* by Cold Play was playing and Maribel found herself humming to the song as she pulled into the Hilton Hotel parking lot. The haunting melody drifted along the airwaves and she listened to the words and started crying.

Foolishly, she had thought that three months was enough time to get over her relationship with Brian, but it still felt like yesterday when he had looked at her with that hurt look in his eyes.

These days when he saw her at church, he gave her a sickly half smile that did not quite reach his eyes, and the truth was it pierced her heart every time she saw it. She hadn't been to church now for the past two weeks. She just couldn't face him and that enigmatic look he had when she came close to him.

These days it seemed as if he had moved on. He had brought Rose to Cathy's wedding and she had had to endure standing up in her bridesmaid dress once again and staring at him as he performed as one of the attendant ministers.

She felt like singing really loudly to the bridge of the song that was playing, as it well reflected her thoughts, '*When the truth is, I miss you so.*'

Whoever, wrote the song was surely privy to her situation. She sniffed as she gazed out into the parking lot. She was in no mood to go to the appreciation party thrown by Lawrence and Rich for their clients and business associates. But Horace had called her and specifically asked her to come. She had reluctantly agreed because it was a wise business move and because Mark and the other partners were going and would fully expect her to come since she managed the account.

Apart from the business obligation, she felt pretty grateful to Horace for standing up for her when she was down. She had grown to like him over the months and couldn't help envying Rose that she had such a great father.

The last chord of the song faded and Maribel checked her face and wiped her eyes delicately with a wet wipe. They looked a little damp but there was no reason that anybody would conclude that she was crying. She checked her dress and smiled vaguely as she locked the car door. She was in a white cocktail dress, which showed a hint more of her upper torso than she normally allowed. It flared out to the ground but had an indecent split at the side, which revealed her nicely toned legs. She had lost a stone since the breakup with Brian, or was it a breakdown.

He had never really come to her and said, "Maribel, it's over." But she was no fool and she was well aware that when a man went out of his way to avoid you for three months that was pretty much it.

She had felt reckless when purchasing the outfit. She had gazed in the mirror of the store and somehow her eyes had blurred and she had imagined that the dress was a white wedding dress and that she was fitting for her wedding. Unfortunately, reality intruded and she had come back to earth, but she had taken the dress anyway. And thought comically that she looked like a virginal ex-whore.

The function was being held on the top floor of the hotel at a suite named the Talk of the Town, which overlooked a good slice of Kingston. Maribel stood in a corner, trying to avoid several persons, including Mark and his beady eyes and Thelma and her superior attitude, but had gotten stuck in a conversation with Michael Rich, a distinguished looking gentleman in his mid-fifties. He had singled her out and was telling her a witty discourse about his efforts to make the track team in high school and then it hit Maribel that he was the other partner, he was Rose's real father. After that sudden realization she had lost her bored posture and had perked up, staring intently at his face, trying to decipher if Rose had any of his features.

She catalogued the similarities and wondered how Thelma slept at night with such a huge secret. Especially when they had been meeting in settings like this for years.

She hadn't realized that her intent attention on Michael had caused him to read her scrutiny as attraction, because he was mumbling under his breath, "I am not single, you know; my wife lives in Miami and my mistress lives in Montego Bay."

Maribel had tuned him out and was nodding yes without hearing what he said.

"But I would really love to go to dinner with you sometime; you are gorgeous. Probably right here in this hotel. They have a lovely restaurant."

She was still musing about the ramifications of Michael being Rose's father and had completely missed what Michael had said.

"She's not interested," said a voice above her head.

She spun around and stared at Brian. He was in a well-cut dinner jacket with a brown open-collar shirt that precisely matched his eyes. He looked so gorgeous and he smelled so good. She closed her eyes briefly so that her brain could register that Brian was here, and he was talking to her or to Michael. She didn't care, but he had a jealous look in his eyes.

"Oh, er, sorry," Michael mumbled, "seems as if I misread things."

Brian nodded and watched as Michael melted into the crowd.

"What on earth am I not interested in?" Maribel asked nervously. "I didn't hear a word he was saying."

Brian shrugged, "I saw you over here completely still, giving him that blank, zoned-out look that you have when you are tuning out someone, and then I saw him stepping closer, so I knew that you were going to be in trouble. He was asking you to dinner."

Maribel smiled, "Well, thanks, I guess."

"He is married," Brian said, shifting on his feet and looking around, "and there is that little commandment about adultery in the Bible."

Maribel nodded again, smiling. What was he doing here?

"I came with Rose," he said, as if he read her mind. "I was ... I mean, I am her date for the evening."

Her eyes clouded over. "So where is she?"

He shrugged; the truth was that Rose ceased to exist the minute he had seen Maribel and though he still felt as if her past was an oozing sore that he couldn't touch, he still felt as he did the first time he saw her—like all the wind had been knocked out of him. He had watched her over the last few months from afar, still stifled by the deep anger that her past life roused up in him.

She cleared her throat. "So how are things?"

He grimaced. "Pretty awful. My father is back in the hospital because of his heart."

Maribel touched his arm. "I am so sorry."

He stiffened; even through his jacket he could feel her touch.

She pulled away her hand as if it was burnt by fire and looked at him with her wide, innocent eyes, and he felt so betrayed. She could touch so many men for money and yet … he slammed a door on those thoughts and looked across the room. It was rapidly filling up and he could see Rose talking and laughing with the same man who had tried to chat up Maribel earlier.

Maribel followed his gaze and looked at Rose in her smart sophisticated outfit and the way she held herself confidently and blurted out, "So how are things with you and Rose? Am I going to get an invitation to the wedding?"

Brian frowned. "She and I are not together."

"Oh," Maribel frowned. "I thought … I saw you two at Cathy's wedding; you looked very close."

Brian remembered the day so well; he had literally felt heart-sore with Maribel standing so near him as part of the bridal party, but he had deliberately kept far from them after his duties as minister was done.

"We aren't together. I wanted to marry somebody else but it turns out she was a …" He clamped his mouth shut and watched as Maribel stiffened in pain.

She turned away from him and he grabbed her arms. "I am sorry, Maribel," he said, tortured. "I knew this would come up … the whole thing is eating me alive …"

She glanced at him, tears in her eyes. "I am leaving now,

excuse me."

He dropped her hand and watched as she walked away and then followed behind.

Maribel stood at the elevator door, waiting for it to take her to the ground level.

"Come on," she whispered and was grateful to see that it was empty when it opened. She went in and was surprised to see that Brian had followed her.

"We have to talk," he sighed, and watched as she pressed the ground floor button.

"So talk." Her voice was choky and suffused with tears.

He grabbed her to him, and they hugged. A deep sigh escaped Maribel.

The door swished open and they broke apart.

Maribel laughed deprecatingly. "I am sorry."

"Me too," Brian said, following her from the elevator. His whole body was tingling from the hug. "I'll follow you to your car."

Maribel nodded and they walked toward the parking lot in silence.

He leaned on her car when they got there and looked at her. "We are both miserable."

Maribel nodded. "I have been miserable for a while."

He sighed. "I still love you."

Maribel gasped.

He turned away. "It's just that I am not sure who I love, Maribel the ideal girl in my head or Maribel the girl with a mammoth past. I don't know if I will ever love Maribel the girl with the past."

"What about just loving Maribel?" Maribel stood in front of him.

He grimaced. "Every time I think about it, Maribel, I feel like smashing something. I have prayed about it, I have tried not to think about it, but I wonder, I say to myself, will I ever trust her with other men? Will I ever know how I compare to all those men and women that she slept with? I am turned off by the fact that even as we speak there are people out there who are watching you have sex on some DVD or still have a picture of you hanging with all your inner secrets exposed for the world to see. Nothing will ever be fresh between us … because you have done it all with a hundred men or more. Will I bore you? Will I constantly wonder how I measure up?"

He paused. "Maribel, look at me."

She looked, tears brimming over onto her cheeks.

"I know you have a relationship with God now, and I am happy about it but your past is almost insurmountable for me. Mainly because of my profession; you see, as a spiritual leader I'm held to a higher standard."

Maribel snorted and turned away. "What about forgiveness? And facing things together? And love?" Her voice petered away.

Brian sighed. "I am no Bible prophet. I am not Hosea, and you are no Gomer. I may want to forgive your past, but it's the forgetting that's the problem. What makes this even worse is that it is so easy to gain access to information these days. I may be preaching somewhere to somebody who has watched my wife in a pornographic movie or seen a nude image of her on the Internet; that won't bode well for the ministry."

Maribel sobbed, "Okay, I get it."

Brian touched her hair and then moved his hands away, balling them into fists.

"Maribel, I am very thankful that Thelma did not blab

about this at church. I thought it was a minor miracle, but I would have to live like this for the rest of my life if we got married, waiting on miracle after miracle that someone would not to find out about your past; for some man that you slept with to declare to the whole world that he had paid the pastor's wife to screw him."

Maribel flinched.

"I am sorry," he sighed and watched as the last vestiges of the evening faded away. "I made a decision yesterday and I thought it only fair to tell you."

Maribel stood, her shoulders hunched, and looked defeated. "What is it?"

"I am going back to Canada at the end of the week. I have already packed. Pastor Green is coming back. He is so happy about it he can barely speak."

Maribel closed her eyes and swallowed. "Okay."

"We would have been good together as a couple," Brian whispered. "I could see us together; I used to even picture our babies. I had many dreams for the both of us."

"I am the same girl you had those dreams about," Maribel said desperately. "I am still who I am in here." She clutched her chest. "I made mistakes when I was younger but I am changed now; I am different. I am older and wiser." She was feverish in her pleading.

Brian shook his head and then squeezed her hand. "This is goodbye, Maribel."

"So is that it," Maribel said harshly. Her belly was flip-flopping weirdly. "Is this really how it will end—you declare that you love me and then you say goodbye?

"Brian, in that book about forgiveness that you are writing you claimed that a mother forgave the man that killed her son. Remember how amazed you were at that?"

Brian nodded, swallowing.

"Well what about this—you, a pastor, and me, an ex-prostitute, getting together despite the odds?"

He turned away. "Goodbye Maribel."

In a last-ditch effort to stop him, Maribel walked behind him, her white dress snagging in her heels and ripping. "Well, I guess that's it, then."

He stopped.

"You are just a preacher, Brian; that's what you do. Preach. Oh, and write. This would have been a good time to practice … you know …" Her voice faded. "Practice what you preach."

She snorted, "But until you know what forgiveness really is, I guess you are the preacher and I will remain a prostitute in your mind's eye."

Brian walked off, leaving her behind with her ripped white dress and her dreams in tatters.

Chapter Twenty-One

It was hard for Maribel to imagine that it had been a year since she joined the choir. Sister Claudia was still as strict as ever, her unlined face stern as she blasted the tuneless modern gospel songs that relied more on beat than pronunciation of words.

It was six months since Brian had left Jamaica, and Maribel couldn't remember a day when she didn't miss him. She couldn't remember a day when she didn't replay "what if" questions in her head about her relationship with Brian and how quickly it turned sour when he found out about her past.

Sister Claudia had the bass section of the choir practicing their piece as she directed them from the piano, and Maribel's mind wandered. She was unhappy and restless, and the melancholy that seemed to dog her days was especially virulent at nights. She got especially restless when Brian sent her a forward in her email inbox. The mails were usually generic and encouraging, sometimes little Bible texts and inspirational stories, and yet when she emailed him he did not respond. At those times she felt especially unhappy.

Rejected.

Unloved.

"Okay choir, I have good news." Sister Claudia faced the choir and smiled briefly. "Our major travelling gig for the year will be to Canada. For some of you newer members, who joined this year we have a major outside of Jamaica travelling experience every year and this year we will be performing at our sister church in Toronto."

A spark of excitement ignited in Maribel. So she would see Brian again. She turned in her seat to look at Cathy. But Cathy was looking slightly under the weather and gave her a wan smile.

"We will be performing on the fourth of March, which I hear is an ideal day because it will be a special one for our previous pastor."

"That's my birthday," Maribel said excitedly.

"Well then," Sister Claudia smiled, "you can do the lead for the song *O Perfect Love.* It was requested by Pastor Brian himself. So we have nearly five months to prepare twelve songs. I don't need to tell you that this will take a while and lots of practice."

Maribel felt tremors race up and down her spine. Why was March fourth a special day for him? Was it because it was her birthday? Was there some secret he was not telling her? Some surprise birthday gift?

He must have been ignoring her for a good reason, so that he could spring a surprise on her when she went to his country.

She went through the rest of choir practice in a daze and afterward cornered a lackluster Cathy in the parking lot.

"Do you understand what this means?" she asked Cathy

excitedly.

Cathy looked at her dully. "What?"

"The Canada trip?" Maribel asked, brimming over with excitement. "He is planning something on my birthday."

Cathy held on to the door of her car and sighed, "Maribel, I have no energy to expend in warning you against getting your hopes up. It's been six months since he left and he hasn't as much as called you. That sounds like finality to me."

"It can't be," Maribel said, frowning. "He will get used to my past and then we will move on."

Cathy sighed, "I think you are being a bit too hopeful."

"Why do you sound like that?" Maribel finally registered that Cathy was looking tired and washed out. "Are you coming down with the flu or something?"

Cathy grinned, "Or something. I should tell my husband first, but hey, you asked. You are going to be an aunt."

Maribel looked at her aghast. "Say what?"

"You heard," Cathy said, grinning.

"Well congrats," Maribel squealed. "I am going to be an aunty. How far along are you? You look like someone slapped you around and then kicked you for good measure; where is the fabled pregnant glow?"

"I am eight weeks preggo," Cathy said, getting in her car. "I just found out today, which means in five months I am not going to be able to go to Canada. Hence, I think I will forgo future choir practices and allow Greg to pamper me in the evenings like a queen."

Maribel smiled. "I was hopeful we could go together."

"There is no way I am going to waddle to Canada at seven months," Cathy grimaced. "Imagine me straining to sing one of Claudia's pieces at this shindig. I guess I will just have to live vicariously through you."

Maribel shrugged. "I have to go. I want to see Brian and

find out what he has planned for us."

Cathy warned, "Maribel, be careful."

"Yes Mama," Maribel said laughingly.

She hugged herself as she approached her car, her mouth in a smile that would not quit. She could see the scenario in her head now; Brian knew she was in the choir so he suggested that they come over on her birthday to sing, just so they could kiss and make up and probably, in the not so distant future, get married and have babies like Cathy and Greg.

She turned up her stereo really high and sang all the way home.

Chapter Twenty-Two

When Maribel checked into the hotel with the rest of the choir members she was floating on cloud nine. She had tried to email Brian over the last few months but he had not responded. All of that added to her suspicion that he was trying to spring a surprise on her and she smiled as she jumped into her spacious bed. She had listened to Dido's *White Flag* while she was on the airplane and now she sat on the bed with a stupid grin on her face. To her it was timeless music and was especially applicable to her now. She sang the second verse out loud.

She had jotted down Brian's number from his email and was now itching to call him; they were supposed to perform at his church tomorrow and at another venue the day after.

She felt anticipation zinging through her. Last year's birthday was a disastrous one for her, and this year—well, this year should be better. How many bad birthdays could a girl take?

She remembered the birthday when Felicia had died. One minute she had stood talking to her friend and the next blood was everywhere, the once-vibrant eyes forever closed.

Then there was the street dance when she had felt so lonely and empty and that bartender had reminded her of her past and of course, last year when Brian found out that she had slept with his uncle.

Now this year was going to be better; she could feel it. She was on Brian's turf now; his country; his surprise. She had deliberately not listened to any of the whisperings about the trip these past five months because she didn't want to inadvertently spoil the surprise. A shaft of unease had pierced her at odd times that he did not call or respond to her emails, only with those generic Bible text emails.

He really was trying to be difficult, she sighed. And her fingers itched as she stared at the telephone. And then she gave in to the temptation. After the operator connected the call she paced the room with the phone on her ear and listened to the rings and then there it was—his voice, his wonderful, honey-toned voice.

"Hello."

"Hey," Maribel said brightly, feeling suddenly gauche and exposed.

Brian inhaled loudly and then exhaled shakily. "Maribel?"

"Yes, it's me," Maribel said huskily.

"I didn't know you were coming with the choir," Brian said hesitantly. "I did ask but Sister Claudia said that she was not going to commit to telling me before everybody was confirmed."

Maribel felt suddenly deflated; he didn't know she was going to be here? All those months of excitement for nothing? She had even done a thorough spa treatment last week so that she could look her best for this imaginary surprise, and he didn't even known she was coming!

"Er ..." She was now at a loss. "I thought you knew," she said lamely.

Brian sighed. "Where are you staying?"

Maribel told him breathlessly.

"I have a gift for you," Brian said. "I might not be able to speak to you tomorrow, so I'll just come over and give it to you now."

He sounded so distant and cold. Maribel actually shivered after she hung up the phone. He said six o'clock; that was five hours away. She curled up on the bed and closed her eyes, all sorts of scenarios running through her head. What was going on? Why couldn't he speak to her tomorrow?

The knock at the door woke up Maribel and she fumbled with a lamp, switching it on before she jerkily got up. My God, she had slept for about four hours. Her mind had churned about the situation for so long that she must have put herself to sleep thinking about it. She glanced at the clock on the night stand and it read 5:57, the flashing red numbers reminding her that she had not even showered or taken the time to get ready.

She peeped through the peephole of the door. It was Brian, looking so fresh and handsome that her breath caught in her throat. She opened the door hurriedly, uncaring about how she looked. She was so excited to see him.

He gazed at her as she drank him in and then he smiled.

"Are you going to let me in?"

Maribel nodded and stepped aside and watched as his broad-shouldered frame passed her and stood into her room looking around.

"This is nice," he swiveled around and looked at her,

"and as usual you look beautiful, a bit sleep tousled but still gorgeous."

He had a package in his hand and he placed it on her bed and then sat down.

Maribel stood up, leaning on the door uncertainly. No hug or kiss or even a warm welcome to Canada. What was going on?

Brian could not believe that he was seeing her in the flesh again after so many months. She was still as beautiful as he remembered, and there she stood with her understated sexuality. He sighed; he had tried to forget her but of course he couldn't. She was the mistake he almost made and desperately wanted to forget.

His hand clenched and he cleared his throat. "My book was published."

Maribel gave him a half smile and said huskily, "That's nice."

The silence stretched between them.

"So how is your father?"

Brian grinned. "As right as rain. My mother takes full credit for that. She has him on a strict vegan diet that seems to be working."

He leaned back comfortably on the bed and Maribel sat tentatively near him. "Why have you never called," she whispered, "or written?"

Brian shrugged, "When I said goodbye, Maribel, I meant it." His gaze raked over her t-shirt and silky pajama shorts.

He swallowed. "I meant every word. I did not want to encourage any more contact between us, so that one or the other of us would be caught up in it."

Maribel tensed up and focused on one side of the room; she wouldn't cry while he was there. She had wasted quite a bit of time in useless hoping and baseless excitement. "So what is the surprise tomorrow then?" she asked hoarsely.

Brian sighed. "I told Sister Claudia that I was getting married and she decided to make a big production out of it."

"Ma-married?" Maribel stumbled. "How? Why? Who?"

"I found the one," Brian said, looking at her crestfallen expression. "Her name is Faith. I thought you knew. I thought Claudia told everyone. I never expected you to come."

Maribel nodded, the knot in her stomach growing tighter and tighter, until a sob escaped her throat.

"Don't cry, Maribel," Brian said soothingly. He was surprised when Maribel started shrieking, a wounded sound like an injured animal.

He went over to her side of the bed and held her. Her warm frame felt so perfect to him and he rubbed her back. But his body was still attracted to her even if his mind was not, and when she turned her tear-stained face into his neck, her lips brushed his ear and she trembled against him.

A riot of suppressed longing engulfed him and he sought her lips and kissed her. So many pent-up emotions went into the kiss: anger over her past and wishful longing that he was marrying her instead of Faith. He punished her in that kiss for not being the woman that he thought she was.

She clung to him and kissed him back fiercely.

Brian felt his self-control snap and all his years of repressing his sexual appetite and facing lust with common sense and God's guidance went up in smoke. He never knew how they ended up naked on that bed. Nor was his intellect engaged at that moment.

When their passion was spent and she gazed at him, a vulnerable look in her eyes, the guilt came roaring at him. He leapt off the bed and started throwing on his clothes. Maribel did not say a word as she watched him frantically dressing. He was whispering, "Oh my God, oh my God."

Strangely, she felt calm and grounded, fulfilled and with a blossoming satisfaction.

"Are you still getting married tomorrow?" she asked him shyly.

"Oh yes," Brian said haltingly. "Maribel, I can't believe that we just did that. I am now a cliché, aren't I?" he said deprecatingly. "I have been so careful through the years to be sexually pure and the night before my wedding, I sleep with somebody else."

Maribel watched him silently.

"I'll have to tell her about this."

"I won't be there tomorrow," Maribel said and turned her naked back to him.

"That's for the best," Brian said, staring at her naked back in fascination. He headed toward the door and then turned back and kissed her on her bare shoulder and walked out.

Maribel went home the next day. On the way home from the airport she opened the package he gave her. It was his book, *Saved and Forgiven.* She opened the first page. *For Maribel;* under that he wrote in pen, *You taught me forgiveness. It was never really my place to forgive; God has already done that for you. It is with utmost weakness that I admit that as a mere man it's the forgetting part that is not very easy. With all my love, Brian.*

She cried all the way home. It would never be resolved, would it? She would always be the prostitute because of her past and he would always be the preacher who chose his ministry over love.

Chapter Twenty-Three

It was Horace who rescued Maribel from her depression.

"Say Maribel," he had called her one Monday, six weeks after the fiasco in Canada, "I suggested your name to Doctor Karen Miekle, a social activist who is desirous of starting a charity to rehabilitate women who are into prostitution."

Maribel had stared at her monitor and paused. "I don't know, Horace."

"I think you should," Horace said lightly. "I think you can do a world of good by showing how you turned your life around and encourage others to do the same. There is nothing better than someone who has beaten the odds, someone who says, 'See what I have done; you can do it too.'"

She had hemmed and hawed and mumbled but Horace had resolutely hammered away at her arguments until finally she had given in.

And that was why she was meeting Karen Miekle at the Sovereign Mall food court. She had a low thrumming in her head that she self-diagnosed as stress. It had been there since her Canada trip. And it just wouldn't go away. The tight tentacles of pain surrounded her head and squeezed whenever she thought about Brian. Sometimes the pain thrummed into the region of her heart. Two weeks ago she had cried like a baby when she had gotten her period; she had so wanted their passionate interlude to result in a child.

She hadn't cared about the added problems that would have created; she had just wanted a piece of Brian with her. She imagined him marrying Faith on her birthday, of all days, and the anger and resentment that she felt toward the unknown Faith had kept her tied up for days.

"Hey Maribel." Karen sat on a bench beside her and sighed, "This is going to be the hottest summer on record. If May can be so bleeding hot, what about July. Lord help us. The sun is out to eat us."

Maribel grinned, staring at the woman beside her incredulously. She sported long sister locks, which were dyed in red yellow and black. Her slim body was encased in tight jeans and she had on a Bob Marley t-shirt.

"Somehow, I was expecting someone looking a bit more doctor-ish," Maribel said aloud.

Karen giggled, "I am a disgrace to the academic establishment and the medical profession."

"I didn't know you were a medical doctor." Maribel looked at her askance.

"Yeah," Karen nodded and reached into her pocket for a gum. "Was a young genius so I got to do my med degree and then a little playing around in sociology."

"Wow," Maribel was impressed, "you don't look a day over twenty."

"You dear girl," Karen squeezed her hand, "I am the ripe old age of twenty-eight."

"I just turned twenty-six," Maribel said contemplatively, "six weeks ago. Bad things happen on my birthday."

Karen grinned. "Bad things happen to me on Valentine's Day. We should share stories and see who is worse off."

"I am," Maribel grimaced, "without even hearing yours."

Karen giggled again. "It was hinted to me that you are interested in working with the rehabilitation of prostitutes and that you would probably have a story to share."

Maribel nodded, biting her lips. She had agonized over the meeting, because in essence she would be laying her life bare for all to examine if she went public with this charity. She was sure that there would be repercussions at work and at church. But somehow, deep in her innermost self, she knew that this was the right thing to do.

If everyone knew, then instead of wondering about who would find out and what would happen, she would in effect just lay it all bare and let the chips fall where they may. Just the very thought of the gut-wrenching year she had dodging from Brian and having Thelma tying her in knots gave her the courage to look at Karen and nod. "I do have a story to share. It's not pretty, though."

Karen nodded. "The important thing is that it's inspiring to others and in sharing it you can impact another person's life for the better."

"Well, are we going to talk here or somewhere more private?"

Karen sighed. "Don't make me leave the relative coolness of this mall right now, I beg of you. Let me tell you a bit about our program first and then we can dash to my office up the road or the building we will be using for our program, which, by the way, has no AC."

Maribel nodded.

"The program is government and UN funded. It is a social

rehabilitation initiative to help our girls and women who have found themselves in the unfortunate situation of prostitution. Not only those women at the roadside but all women who engage in sex for money. We are talking education initiatives, skills training, and workshops, which is where you will come in, and of course medical interventions."

"Sounds interesting," Maribel said.

"We will house them, find jobs for them and send them out into the workplace. We want to empower the women in the oldest profession, if you know what I mean," Karen winked at her.

"I was once involved in prostitution," Maribel said seriously, "so I know what you mean."

Karen sighed. "If we had a program like this for young women going a long time ago, I am sure things would have been different for you, wouldn't they?"

"Oh yes," Maribel curled her fingers on her bag strap, "I would probably be married by now without my damn past hanging over my head."

"Man problems?" Karen queried, raising her brows.

"He is a pastor," Maribel said dejectedly, "married by now, so I guess that's it for my foolish dreams of living happily ever after with him."

Karen patted her hand. "Somehow, I sense that platitudes like 'you will move on one day,' and 'you deserve better' won't work here."

Maribel shook her head.

"Well then, let's get your mind on something else. I think we should tour the facility that we are going to be getting after years of lobbying the government. I am going to personally beg for an air conditioning unit for the offices, or I won't be able to function."

Chapter Twenty-Four

Her heart was not broken anymore; it was barely patched up in places but not broken. She appeared on television with Karen, advocating for the charity organization. They featured her on talk shows, where she told her story. They even did a full spread on her in two newspapers.

She resigned from Fisher and Smith on a Wednesday because she got a job offer to work with UNICEF as an accountant starting the following Tuesday. They never said a word about her past and though she got curious looks at the office after her first televised interview, nobody treated her any differently, and a large part of that had to do with the fact that a new story—even more amazing than her past— was brewing. It was the talk of the office; Mark Ellington was being investigated for embezzlement. In the accounting world that trumped ex-prostitution any day.

People were more interested in her opinion on the embezzlement than her days as a prostitute. Vivian was happy for her, but sad that she was leaving.

She stuck her head around the office door every five minutes. "What am I going to do, Maribel? Who am I going to have lunch with now that your new office is at the other end of town? Though I love you, I can't see myself battling the midday traffic just to eat with you and come back."

Maribel would smile wickedly. "Weren't you the one who convinced me to apply for the job?"

"Yup," Vivian said contritely. "I thought the pay was better and the change of environment was well needed. But things are different now; Monster Mark is now on his way out with Mr. Fisher and Smith's boot in his backside."

Maribel grinned. "When he calls you to his office you must answer, 'Yes Mr. Embezzler, Sir.'"

Church was another matter for Maribel. The harshest of critics attended church, everyone knew that, and that was why she regrettably had to leave the choir.

"For a season," Sister Claudia had told her angrily. "I can't understand why. It is still the same you, and I need your voice for my next song."

Maribel had touched her hand sympathetically.

Sister Bertram had sidled up to them and said sternly, "I will resist any attempts to block you from Women's Ministries meetings so you better be there on Sunday; you need our strength now more than ever."

Cathy was eight months pregnant and huge with it. She was no longer an ally at Women's Ministries because she laughingly told Maribel that she could barely waddle to her own bathroom, much less church.

So Maribel faced the wrath of the church sisters and the awkward suggestions from her church brothers alone—when they realized that she was not amused by their barefaced attempts at propositioning her, she was eventually left alone.

Thelma was instrumental in her being left alone; she refused to gossip about Maribel, to the point where she would snap at anyone who brought up the matter to her. Misconstruing her defensiveness as support, many persons began to view Maribel in a positive light.

Her story could happen to anyone was the philosophical spin that was thrown around. And what was once the indefensible now was defended with single-minded determination.

Time had indeed taken care of her story. And slowly she was just another church sister with a very interesting past. She received so many dinner invitations from her church brethren that she jokingly told Cathy that she was going to have to hire a social secretary.

And then another birthday rolled around. Maribel was sitting in her office answering mail when one caught her eye. Happy Birthday was in the subject line and it was from Brian.

Her fingers trembled when she clicked the message.

Hi Maribel,

I learned something since your last birthday— I am human and fallible. I have ideals that sometimes shatter and leave me very miserable in the smithereens of my broken emotions. I would like to think sometimes that because I follow the rules as outlined by the Bible, that I am close to God, but I realized that it's when I take self out of the equation and just allow God to lead, that is when I am really close to him. For the past year, I have prayed for just that, selflessness.

This letter is an apology of sorts. Last year I hurt you, I know that. I wanted to at the time. I wanted you to feel as low and as shattered as I was feeling. Remember the texts from Corinthians that I used to send to you, one verse at a time? Well I read them again today and I realized that even though I professed to love you, I was the opposite of those things when the first obstacle presented itself in my idyllic vision of the two of us.

I am sorry, Maribel. I am sorry that it took me a year to grow up and to realize that I still love you. I can't shake it, this feeling, this principle, this emotion. I tried to shake it; I tried to marry another woman, convinced myself that she was 'the one'. She had such a pristine, clean past and was the antithesis of everything Maribel that I think I went crazy for a while. I am sure you heard that the wedding was called off—couldn't do it. I would have been punishing her for my unhappiness.

So I beg your forgiveness for hurting you further. I don't care anymore about your past, Maribel. As I see it I have two choices, you and your past or living alone. I think I will take you—if you will have me, that is.

Maribel had to close her office door before she rested her head on the desk and sobbed, loud choking sobs that she didn't care if anyone heard. It was grief and relief, a combination that meant she was also laughing when she read the lines, *I am sure you heard that the wedding was called off.* No, she hadn't heard.

She didn't want to hear anything that had to do with Brian after that Canada trip. *So he isn't married.*

She sat up straighter in her chair. *I don't care anymore about your past, Maribel. As I see it I have two choices, you and your past or alone. I think I will take you—if you will have me, that is.*

Oh Lord, thank you, she sobbed happily. *Thank you so much. Thank you for being my friend through all this. Thank you for loving me so much that you never gave up on me even when I was wayward.*

She had to compose herself for a long while before she could write Brian. Tears just kept streaming down her face and she left them unchecked. 'Thank you God' just seemed so inadequate right now.

"Father, this is the best birthday ever," she whispered as she typed, her hands flying over the keys.

Hi Brian,

I'll take you.

She waited impatiently around her monitor, completely ignoring her telephone ringing until the incessant rings made her grab the receiver aggressively.

"Yes." Her voice was clipped and impatient.

"Thank you." His voice was husky.

"How did you know I was not with Fisher and Smith anymore?" Maribel whispered hoarsely.

"Vivian told me."

"Oh." She was tongue-tied.

"How about lunch?" He had a smile in his voice.

"How? Where? When?" Maribel was so surprised her heart was beating a mile a minute.

"I got in last night for your birthday," Brian said smoothly. "I always wanted to propose on your birthday."

"Yes," Maribel said eagerly.

"Yes what?" Brian asked, puzzled.

"Yes, I'll marry you." Maribel started shoving her things

in her bag. She was definitely going to spend the day with him.

"Thank God for that, but I am still going to ask properly," Brian said. "What time should I pick you up for lunch?"

"Now," Maribel demanded.

"It is eight-thirty in the morning," Brian laughed. "I will be there in ten minutes."

Maribel couldn't stop smiling.

Epilogue

"**I**sn't it crass and completely lacking in taste to print as a headline *The Preacher and The Prostitute Tie the Knot?*" Brian's mother, Catherine, was pacing around the room as she rocked Cathy's four-month-old baby Matthew to sleep and glancing disdainfully at the newspaper headline.

Vivian was lounging on the bed, a mirror propped on her knee as she applied her eyeliner carefully. "I like that word crass. I must use it next time Paul's mother comes to Jamaica."

"That's next month," Maribel said pointedly, "for your wedding." She was in a white slip and nothing else; the wedding was not going to start for another hour.

"I like it," Cathy said, pinning up her hair. "The Preacher and the Prostitute has a nice ring to it."

"The Preacher and the ex-Prostitute would be even better for our charity." Karen was in the corner reading a copy of the paper. "And look, the critters spelled my surname incorrectly.

It says here 'Maribel Contrell, soon to be Edwards, a former prostitute who is an accountant with UNICEF and a motivational speaker for the charity organization Women Unite, has decided to tie the knot with popular Canadian pastor Brian Edwards. Her close friend and head of Women Unite, Karen Meekle'—they spelt my name MEEKLE? Can you believe it?"

"Read more," Cathy mumbled, "I am sure my name has to be mentioned."

Karen cleared her throat. "Her close friend and head of Women Unite, Doctor Karen Miekle, says that Maribel's marriage will create a huge gap when she leaves for Canada next month. 'She was our best motivational speaker, the best example of what women can achieve when they decide to empower themselves from the shackles of prostitution.'"

"Read about me," Cathy said. "They must mention me."

Karen snorted. "Cathy Norwood, Maribel's best friend ..."

"Nuh uh," Vivian retorted. "I am Maribel's best friend."

"I knew her first," Cathy spun around from the mirror. "I introduced her to God."

Catherine cleared her throat before Vivian could retort. "Ladies, ladies. Before your argument gets louder, I am going to put this little one down with his grandmother," she indicated a drowsy Matthew, "and I will be back to referee, so freeze there for a while."

Maribel giggled. "You guys are ridiculous; you are all my closest friends and I can't imagine my big day without you three. And to tell you the truth, I am kinda dreading going to Canada without you all."

Vivian sniffed and got off the bed. Cathy and Karen walked to her and hugged her.

"You will be with the man you love; we are happy for you." Vivian squeezed her and then glanced in the mirror.

"My dratted eye makeup is now on my cheeks."

They laughed together and were still chuckling when a knock sounded on the door. Karen opened the door and then giggled, "Ladies, the preacher has sent a gift."

Karen handed a small glass bottle to Maribel. It contained a neatly wrapped scroll. She took it and opened up the paper and read out loud. "If I speak in the languages of men and of angels but have not love I am a resounding gong or a clanging cymbal ... Love is patient. Love is kind. It does not envy, it does not boast, it is not proud, it is not rude, it is not self-seeking, it is not easily angered, it keeps no record of wrongs. Love does not delight in evil but rejoices in the truth. It always protects, always trusts, always hopes, always perseveres. Love never fails. I love you, Maribel."

And with tears all dried and Maribel resplendent in her off-white wedding dress, she glided through the pews, her attendants behind her as she stared at Brian—his handsome face wreathed in smiles. She placed her hands in his and whispered, "I love you too."

THE END

Keep reading for an excerpt from *Private Sins.*

First Book in the Three Rivers Series.

"I can't do this anymore," Kelly said, looking at Chris with guilt in her eyes.

He was driving along the scenic coastline of Runaway Bay, heading towards his villa. He flinched and tightened his hand on the steering wheel and in a voice belying his tension, asked gently, "You can't do what? You can't be my interior decorator anymore?"

"Be your mistress, girlfriend, bit-on-the-side. Whatever this is, Chris," Kelly replied, glancing at him pleadingly. "This is wrong; so wrong on many levels." She clasped her hands in her lap and inhaled. "It should not have started."

"You love me," he said, slowing down the vehicle and turning into the villa's entrance. The landscaping was still unfinished and some men were busy constructing a stone wall. Chris tooted them as he navigated up the meandering driveway. The landscaper, who was transplanting a palm tree, waved to him.

He stopped under the overhang at the front entrance; already the landscaper had planted white roses beside the trellis. They were supposed to entwine around the posts and create a scenic point of interest.

He tried to avoid Kelly's startled look as he got out of the car, slamming the door harder than he should.

Kelly scrambled out of the car and walked around to his side quickly.

"No, I don't. I don't think I do. This is just a fling, remember? We agreed, six months ago, when this whole thing started, that it would just be a one off. Chris...Chris! Are you listening to me?"

Chris strolled into the villa and headed straight for his temporary office, which a suite of rooms behind the receptionist area.

Kelly swiftly walked in after him, her high heels making

an echo on the marble tiles. The lobby area was the last place that she had to decorate and furnish, then she would be done with the job. She had done the ten two-bedroom villas that Chris had commissioned her to do, and in the process had lost all sense of morality.

This job had been her moral undoing.

She winced when she thought about how many days she spent in this very space with Chris Donahue in a sensual haze—hiding away from the real world, and lying to herself and her family.

She leaned against the reception desk. It was not yet varnished, but the furniture maker had finished the design to her dictates. It would perfectly complement the forest theme she had envisioned when she had first seen the space.

She glanced in the mirrors that lined the wall in front of the desk and tried to avoid looking at herself. Her reflection seemed slightly accusing and her heartfelt sigh echoed into the hollow room. She cupped her hand under her chin and a rush of guilt—so raw and suffocating—grasped her by the chest that she found that she was breathing shallowly.

She heard the door behind the desk open. The whole wall was covered in wood and the door was a seamless addition. She glanced around to see Chris standing there with a wounded look in his eyes.

"I don't want to end this," he whispered pleadingly.

Kelly sighed. "I know, but it has to."

Chris ran his fingers through his curly hair and leaned against the door. "You could get a divorce…marry me."

Kelly inhaled then exhaled rapidly. "I have two children, Chris! That decision would have far-reaching consequences."

"I can take care of all of you," Chris said earnestly, now standing before her—his hazel eyes glistening with tears.

Kelly looked away from him and shook her head. "I still

love my husband. I don't think I ever stopped loving him."

Her words stood between them and he backed away slightly. "He doesn't give you the love and attention that you crave. I have watched you both over the years. He is so involved with his job that you are a mere second in his affections. I am a property developer. We could build hotels and villas together and you decorate them. We complement each other. You love me too, Kelly! I know you do. I can see you are trying to fight it because of some misplaced loyalty to a husband who doesn't care about you. If you went missing, he wouldn't care."

"That's not true," Kelly said, sobbing. "I can't just throw away ten years and two kids because of lust! I can't. I won't!"

"Lust!" Chris snorted. "I have loved you for longer than ten years. The sad part about this is that you knew, but you married him anyway. I wasn't good enough for you then and apparently I am not good enough for you now."

"Chris...don't." Kelly wiped her eyes and gave him a beseeching look. "I am sorry, okay. I am sorry, sorrier than you would ever know. I'm sorry that this whole thing escalated into what it is now. You are handsome and young and rich. You will find somebody and..."

"Shut up!" Chris shouted. "Just shut up! You accepted this job willingly, Kelly. For years you refused whenever I asked you to work on a project with me because you knew how I felt about you. You have always felt the tension between us. You wanted to start this affair. You wanted a reason to leave your relationship. Here I am Kelly! Here's the reason!"

Chris jabbed himself in the chest, a stormy glint in his eyes. "Leave Theo and come to me. I am not marrying anyone else. I am not interested in anyone else."

Kelly turned away from him, her eyes damp. "I am choosing my family, Chris. Please, just take me home. Drat it, I wish I had driven my car. I will try to finish up the lobby in the agreed time, but I am putting an end to this now. Can we please not discuss this affair again?"

"We'll see about that." Chris stormed toward the car. "You can't just use me and then dump me! I love you."

Kelly walked behind him. "You can't tell him, Chris. He's your pastor! You are his first elder! The church would have a field day with this if it ever gets out. Please see reason."

Chris slammed the car door, and Kelly had to hobble fast to get in before he drove off.

OTHER BOOKS BY BRENDA BARRETT

Love Triangle Series

Love Triangle: Three Sides To The Story - George, the husband, Marie, the wife and Karen-the mistress. They all get to tell their side of the story.

Love Triangle: After The End - Torn between two lovers. Colleen married her high school sweetheart, Isaiah, hoping that they would live happily ever after but life intruded and Isaiah disappeared at sea. She found work with the rich and handsome, Enrique Lopez, as a housekeeper and realized that she couldn't keep him at arms length...

Love Triangle: On The Rebound - For Better or Worse, Brandon vowed to stay with Ashley, but when worse got too much he moved out and met Nadine. For the first time in years he felt happy, but then Ashley remembered her wedding vows...

New Song Series

Going Solo (New Song Series-Book 1)- Carson Bell, had a lovely voice, a heart of gold, and was no slouch in the looks department. So why did Alice abandon him and their daughter? What did she want after ten years of silence?

Duet on Fire (New Song Series- Book 2)- Ian and Ruby had problems trying to conceive a child. If that wasn't enough, her ex-lover the current pastor of their church wants her back...

Tangled Chords (New Song Series- Book 3)- Xavier Bell, the poor, ugly duckling has made it rich and his looks have been incredibly improved too. Farrah Knight, hotel heiress had cruelly rejected him in the past but now she needed help. Could Xavier forgive and forget?

Broken Harmony(New Song Series-Book 4)- Aaron Lee, wanted the top job in his family company but he had a moral clause to consider just when Alka, his married ex-girlfriend walks back into his life.

A Past Refrain (New Song Series-Book 5) - Jayce had issues with forgetting Haley Greenwald even though he had a new woman in his life. Will he ever be able to shake his love for Haley?

Perfect Melody (New Song Series- Book 6) - Logan Moore had the perfect wife, Melody but his secretary Sabrina was hell bent on breaking up the family. Sabrina wanted Logan whatever the cost and she had a secret about Melody, that could shatter Melody's image to everyone.

The Bancroft Family Series

Homely Girl (The Bancrofts- Book 0) - April and Taj were opposites in so many ways. He was the cute, athletic boy that everybody wanted to be friends with. She was the overweight, shy, and withdrawn girl. Do April and Taj have a love that can last a lifetime? Or will time and separate paths rip them apart?

Saving Face (The Bancrofts- Book 1) - Mount Faith University drama begins with a dead president and several suspects including the president in waiting Ryan Bancroft.

Tattered Tiara (The Bancrofts- Book 2) - Micah Bancroft is targeted by femme fatale Deidra Durkheim. There are also several rape cases to be solved.

Private Dancer (The Bancrofts- Book 3) Adrian Bancroft was gutted when he returned to Jamaica and found out that his first and only love Cathy Taylor was a stripper and was literally owned by the menacing drug lord, Nanjo Jones.

Goodbye Lonely (The Bancrofts- Book 4) - Kylie Bancroft was shy and had to resort to going to confidence classes. How could she win the love of Gareth Beecher, her faculty adviser, a man with a jealous ex-wife in his past and a current mystery surrounding a hand found in his garden?

Practice Run (The Bancrofts Book 5) - Marcus Bancroft had many reasons to avoid Mount Faith but Deidra Durkheim was not one of them. Unfortunately, on one of his visits he was the victim of a deliberate hit and run.

Sense of Rumor (The Bancrofts- Book 6) - Arnella Bancroft was the wild, passionate Bancroft, the creative loner who didn't mind living dangerously; but when a terrible thing happened to her at her friend Tracy's party, it changed her. She found that courting rumors can be devastating and that only the truth could set her free.

A Younger Man (The Bancrofts- Book 7) - Pastor Vanley Bancroft loved Anita Parkinson despite their fifteen-year age gap, but Anita had a secret, one that she could not reveal to Vanley. To tell him would change his feelings toward her, or force him to give up the ministry that he loved so much.

Just To See Her (The Bancrofts- Book 8) - Jessica Bancroft had the opportunity to meet her fantasy guy Khaled, he was finally coming to Mount Faith but she had feelings for Clay Reid, a guy who had all the qualities she was looking for. Who would she choose and what about the weird fascination Khaled had for Clay?

The Three Rivers Series

Private Sins (Three Rivers Series-Book 1) - Kelly, the first lady at Three Rivers Church was pregnant for the first elder of her church. Could she keep the secret from her husband and pretend that all was well?

Loving Mr. Wright (Three Rivers Series- Book 2) - Erica saw one last opportunity to ditch her single life when Caleb Wright appeared in her town. He was perfect for her, but what was he hiding?

Unholy Matrimony (Three Rivers Series- Book 3) - Phoebe had a problem, she was poor and unhappy. Her solution to marry a rich man was derailed along the way with her feelings for Charles Black, the poor guy next door.

If It Ain't Broke (Three Rivers Series- Book 4) - Chris Donahue wanted a place in his child's life. Pinky Black just wanted his love. She also wanted him to forget his obsession with Kelly and love her. That shouldn't be so hard? Should it?

Contemporary Romance/Drama

New Beginnings - Inner city girl Geneva was offered an opportunity of a lifetime when she found out that her 'real' father was a very wealthy man. Her decision to live up-town meant that she had to leave Froggie, her 'ghetto don,' behind. She also found herself battling with her stepmother and battling her emotions for Justin, a suave up-towner.

Full Circle - After graduating from university, Diana wanted to return to Jamaica to find her siblings. What she didn't foresee was that she would meet Robert Cassidy and that both their pasts would be intertwined, and that disturbing questions would pop up about their parentage, just when they were getting close.

Historical Fiction/Romance

The Empty Hammock - Workaholic, Ana Mendez, fell asleep in a hammock and woke up in the year 1494. It was the time of the Tainos, a time when life seemed simpler, but Ana knew that all of that was about to change.

The Pull Of Freedom - Even in bondage the people, freshly arrived from Africa, considered themselves free. Led by Nanny and Cudjoe the slaves escaped the Simmonds' plantation and went in different directions to forge their destiny in the new country called Jamaica.

Jamaican Comedy (Material contains Jamaican dialect)

Di Taxi Ride And Other Stories - Di Taxi Ride and Other

Stories is a collection of twelve witty and fast paced short stories. Each story tells of a unique slice of Jamaican life.

Withdrawn

CPSIA information can be obtained at www.ICGtesting.com
Printed in the USA
LVOW11s1951280416

485790LV00001B/15/P

9 789769 528765